"You're taking too much into your own hands."

Paige turned to face Chad on the veranda. "Something isn't right."

"Look, Paige, it's all perfectly legal." Chad sighed and walked a few steps away. "Your aunts needed a decent boat to travel back and forth to Brunswick and St. Simon's in. That old scow of theirs could barely make it to—"

"I agree a new boat is necessary. But if you spent their money without their knowledge, how do you do it? By whose authority?"

"They didn't know they were getting a new boat, that's true. But you agree they'll be delighted with it, don't you?"

"Yes, but—"

"Don't worry about your aunts' money," Chad said. "I assure you everything is under control."

But whose control, Paige wondered unhappily. . . .

WELCOME
TO THE WONDERFUL WORLD
OF *Harlequin Romances*

Interesting, informative and entertaining,
each Harlequin Romance portrays an appealing
and original love story. With a varied array
of settings, we may lure you on an African safari,
to a quaint Welsh village, or an exotic Riviera
location—anywhere and everywhere that adventurous
men and women fall in love.

As publishers of Harlequin Romances, we're
extremely proud of our books. Since 1949,
Harlequin Enterprises has built its publishing
reputation on the solid base of quality and
originality. Our stories are the most popular
paperback romances sold in North America; every
month, six new titles are released and sold at
nearly every book-selling store in Canada and the
United States.

For a list of all titles currently available,
send your name and address to:

HARLEQUIN READER SERVICE,
(In the U.S.) P.O. Box 52040, Phoenix, AZ 85072-2040
(In Canada) P.O. Box 2800, Postal Station A
5170 Yonge Street, Willowdale, Ont. M2N 5T5

We sincerely hope you enjoy reading
this Harlequin Romance.

Yours truly,

THE PUBLISHERS
Harlequin Romances

Touch of Gold

Pamela Browning

Harlequin Books

TORONTO · NEW YORK · LONDON
AMSTERDAM · PARIS · SYDNEY · HAMBURG
STOCKHOLM · ATHENS · TOKYO · MILAN

Original hardcover edition published in 1984
by Mills & Boon Limited

ISBN 0-373-02659-5

Harlequin Romance first edition December 1984

CHAPTER ONE

THE late afternoon sunshine touched Paige's face with gold; inhaling deeply, letting the pungent sea air dispel the odours of the city that clung to her skirt and blazer, she swept her eyes over the blue water and the wind-ruffled marsh grass beyond. No sign of Aunt Biz in her little motorboat. With a twinge of exasperation she wondered if the aunts had received her letter.

If they hadn't, of course, she'd be stranded here at the lonely private boat dock on St Simons Island. She'd have to walk back into the village and try to find someone—anyone—who could give her a lift to St Albans.

She sighed and adjusted the flowing citron-and-green paisley scarf around her neck. Her softly pleated lightweight yellow wool skirt flapped disconcertingly around her knees in the wind, showing a bit too much leg. Even though there was no one around, Paige leaned over and futilely tried to anchor the skirt at a more modest length. Giving up, she considered removing her jacket, finally deciding against it even though the May sunshine was becoming increasingly warm. The jacket would be just one more thing to transfer to Aunt Biz's boat. When she came. *If* she came. With a feeling of discouragement, Paige sat down precariously on her largest suitcase. For the sake of comfort, she unbuttoned one more button on her silk blouse and wondered if this trip was worth the bother.

Her feeling of unrest had been building since last October when Aunt Sophie had written about the young live-in handyman she and Aunt Biz had found to help them repair the house. Good, Paige had thought at the time, they *need* someone to take care of that big old barn of a place. After all, they had been living alone there for a good ten years, ever since Uncle John had died, and the house hadn't been in very good shape then.

But subsequent letters had, while raving about how wonderful Chad the handyman was, given Paige cause for alarm. Chad was so kind to them, but when the plumbing had broken down he hadn't known what to do. Chad was extremely handsome, but when he had tried to change the rusty old locks on the doors, he'd botched the job and they'd had to fetch a locksmith over from St Simons. Aunt Sophie and even Aunt Biz had treated all this as though it was funny, neglecting to reply to Paige's uneasy comments in her letters.

Privately Paige thought they had better get themselves a new handyman, but she didn't start to become truly alarmed until she began to think more and more about the two elderly ladies living on isolated St Albans Island with this Chad, who was evidently some stray boat bum they'd picked up when his boat had been stranded along the Intracoastal Waterway.

Who was he, anyway? Both Aunt Biz and Aunt Sophie had ignored this question in her letters. Paige's concern about her aunts coincided with a problem in her own personal life, a problem that needed time and distance to put it into perspective. So when she had been able to arrange an indefinite leave of absence from the airline, she wrote to the aunts and told them when to expect her. And here she was, looking for Aunt Biz who, without the convenience of a telephone, could not even be reached to be told Paige was waiting for her.

She watched several large pleasure craft cruise by on the Intracoastal Waterway, a mostly inland, easily navigable safe passage for boats which stretched from Massachusetts to Florida. Here at St Simons Island, one of the Golden Isles between the Intracoastal and the Atlantic Ocean off the coast of Georgia, sailors on the waterway were treated to an ever-changing panorama of marsh and sea and sky. Perhaps because of the very spaciousness of the surroundings, or the state of mind caused by it, every colour and every sound seemed magnified, reflected and reflected again in the huge mirrored expanse of water. And on St Albans, the smaller private island where the aunts lived, feelings seemed intensified by its very remoteness. At least it had always seemed that way to Paige.

How long had it been since she had visited St Albans? Paige had to think for a moment. It would have been five years ago, just before she had enrolled in college as a freshman. Shortly afterwards her mother, Aunt Sophie's and Aunt Biz's niece Elisabeth, the daughter of the only aunt to leave St Albans and marry, had died following a long painful illness.

Paige had spent an intensely sad summer here then, trying to pull herself together and decide what to do with her life. After Mother's hospital bills had been paid, there hadn't been enough money left to finance her college education. But the aunts, her great-aunts really, had intervened. Aunt Biz, who managed the aunts' considerable fortune, had insisted on paying Paige's way through the University of California. Paige would always be greatful to them for that. And if now, in their old age, they needed help, she would do whatever she had to do. Besides, she loved them dearly.

Lost in her reverie, she didn't hear the boat approaching at first. But then there was no mistaking it—the tinny knock-knock of the ancient motor on the *Marsh Mallow*, the aunts' rusty old skiff.

She stood up and joyfully waved both hands at the tiny boat approaching in the distance. She had begun to doubt that they were going to come for her at all. But there was dauntless Aunt Biz sitting in the stern of the boat and wearing her blue captain's hat.

Only something was wrong. It wasn't Aunt Biz who sat in the boat, ploughing a wide white wake through the calm waters of the Intracoastal. Aunt Biz was lean, yes, but not muscular; Aunt Biz didn't have broad shoulders, nor did she incline herself forward like that, one elbow on her knee as she steered. And the hair that blew back from the edges of the blue cap was tawny fair, golden in the sun, not Aunt Biz's familiar straight grey mop. As the boat drew closer, Paige realised who it must be. Chad Smith, the itinerant handyman.

He aimed the boat at the dock and pulled it expertly alongside. With disregard for her expensive suit, he threw her a line that had been lying in the water in the bottom of the boat and said, 'Here, toss this over that piling for me, will you?' The motor coughed as he shut it off.

He leaped to the dock and stood regarding her with a half smile, apparently liking what he saw. 'Paige Brownell?' he said, and his voice was low and pleasing.

'Yes,' she said, caught off her guard. She hadn't been prepared for someone so distractingly masculine, so rakishly handsome. He stood with his thumbs hooked in the belt loops of his faded blue jeans, gazing lazily down at her through half-closed eyelids. His look, long and languid, slid from her eyes to her mouth, where it lingered as sensuously as a forbidden caress. Paige felt her tongue involuntarily moisten her parted lips; he raised his eyebrows in quick interest and let his eyes drift possessively down her curvaceous figure, skimming, for the moment, over her high round breasts pressed tautly against the fabric of her jacket, resting briefly at her slim waist, hovering appraisingly on her softly rounded hips, then travelling swiftly to her well-shaped legs. He stroked his eyes the length of her body, which was now tight with unexpected tension, responding involuntarily to the aggressive scrutiny of this man.

His visual caress came to rest boldly on the low neckline of her silk blouse, unbuttoned to an almost immodest level. She felt a warm flush of excitement rising from the soft fullness of her breasts to her throat, finally suffusing her cheeks with an unaccustomed blush. Chad Smith noticed her embarrassment and favoured her with a roguish grin, which only disconcerted her more. She felt as though every nerve in her body was exposed to his devastating eyes.

He removed his thumbs from his belt loops and thrust his right hand forward. 'Chad Smith,' he said.

Paige hesitantly extended her own small hand, which he enveloped in his larger one. 'How do you do?' she said, wondering if her equilibrium had deserted her. Her hand, clasped in his, was actually trembling.

He leaned back and looked at her, a sharp, teasing look. 'This isn't a proper welcome for you. Aunt Biz said to take care of this matter exactly as she would do. And I have a good idea that she would have done this.'

Without warning he swept her into his strong, sinewy, suntanned arms and planted a much too enthusiastic kiss on her lips. His mouth was warm and alluring and tasted of salt; Paige could feel the play of hard muscles in his chest as he held her too closely. Suddenly his kiss, which was begun in something akin to jest, changed in character. His lips, at first hard and passionless, took on a disposition of their own, not soft, but supple, not gentle, but seductive. They moved against hers with a studied effect, eliciting the most exquisite sensations.

Against her will, Paige found herself responding to their incredible sweetness. Her lips accommodated to his as though she had been kissing him all her life; the fit was perfect. His arms enclosed her, pressing her to him in a powerful embrace that made it all but impossible for her to breathe. And he was intensifying the kiss, deepening it, asking for more, much more, than she was willing to give. Finally he released her abruptly and stood looking coolly down at her without a word.

Paige gasped in defiant outrage and then, concern for her aunts overriding any sense of propriety, she caught her breath and asked quickly, accusingly, 'Aunt Biz and Aunt Sophie—are they all right?'

'Fit as two fiddles, and full of fiddle-faddle,' he said, grinning nonchalantly as he turned away from her and swung her two suitcases into the skiff. Why, the nerve of it! He was acting as though nothing had happened!

He went on, 'Aunt Biz was all set to fetch you, but the boat motor wouldn't catch, and then Aunt Sophie came running out on the dock with some wild tale about a pot that was boiling over, and Aunt Biz abandoned the motor-repair project and awarded it to me. She and Aunt Sophie are still trying to un-boil the pot.' No matter what his effect had been on her, there was no evidence whatever that she had had a corresponding effect on him. At least the aunts were safe; Chad's story about the pot boiling over sounded typically like both Farrier aunts.

His casual manner infuriated her after his forceful and demanding liberties. Still, she didn't know what to do about it. She stood watching him as he stowed her suitcases in the skiff, admiring, in spite of herself, the ripple of his muscles straining beneath his thin clinging knit shirt.

One part of her longed to retreat along the dock and walk—no, run—back to the village, where she might or might not be able to find someone to transport her to St Albans Island. Yet the other part of her, the Paige who had been travelling all day, was so weary that she longed to see her aunts, longed to rest and put her feet up and be coddled.

There were only two choices, really. She could get in the skiff with this man, or she could not. Much as she would have preferred to find her own way to St Albans, leaving him now would probably create more problems than it would solve. First, there was the sticky wicket of finding transportation to the island, never an easy proposition. If no one could take her there, she would have to spend the night at a hotel, and her suitcases were already stashed in the *Marsh Mallow*. Then there was the worry of Chad Smith going back to her aunts and telling them that she had refused to get in the boat with him. Whatever would they think?

Finally her common sense won out. She would go with Chad Smith, but she would keep her distance. She warily accepted Chad's proffered hand and climbed down into the boat, sitting gingerly in the bow on a seat that was damp with spray.

'I can't guarantee that this motor will start,' he warned her, pulling on the starter. The motor, ever unreliable, groaned and died. Paige raised her eyebrows in concern, but Chad Smith grinned at her with what she supposed was meant to be reassurance. He pulled again, and this time the motor whirred and caught, filling the air with acrid fumes.

'Is there something seriously wrong with it?' Paige asked, raising her voice to be heard over the noise.

'Undoubtedly,' said Chad, acting as though the motor's ills didn't concern him. But as the handyman, you'd think he'd *do* something about the motor, thought Paige. The boat and its motor were the aunts' only link to the outside world, living as they did on their secluded island.

Undaunted, Chad pushed off from the dock and turned the *Marsh Mallow* northward. They headed past the northern edge of St Simons Island, fringed with waist-high marsh grass, broad-bladed and green. They rounded the tip of Little St Simons, a private island very much like St Albans but larger.

Chad steered the boat eastward towards the sea, and ahead of them Paige saw her initial glimpse of St Albans. As always, she thrilled to her first view of the island.

Like the other Golden Isles, it was bordered with lush green marsh grass. Beyond the marshland the island rose above sea level, deeply forested with moss-draped live oaks. Inland was what the family had always called the Manse, the big two-storey house that had been home to generations of Paige's ancestors since the first, a French Huguenot, had established a cotton plantation on the island some two hundred years ago. And beyond the marshes and the tangled forests and the wide white sandy beach was the Atlantic Ocean. If there was ever a paradise on earth, Paige thought, it was scenic St Albans.

She had been facing front in the bow, watching for the island, letting the wind whip her dark brown hair back from her face. But now, curious, she turned towards Chad Smith, and from under the cover of her eyelashes, she studied him surreptitiously, this time concentrating on the details that she had missed because of their most unorthodox greeting.

He was a tall man, wide-shouldered and strong, and his skin was tanned dark by the sun. An outdoor man, one at home with boats, at ease at the tiller. Too, he was older than she had been led to expect—the aunts had referred to him as a boy, yet she would judge him to be in his early thirties. His hair under the breezy blue cap was lighter than she had at first thought, bleached several different shades of blond by the sun and salt air. His eyebrows were thick, also lightened by the sun, and his lashes were long and sandy. Beneath the lashes his eyes, an uncommon shade of amber flecked with brown—or were they brown flecked with amber?—were alert as they scanned the horizon.

The roar of the motor, punctuated by a series of ominous knocks, precluded conversation, so Paige swivelled back around and looked towards St Albans. All at once, she felt selfconscious about the way she looked. She should have tied her lustrous hair back with her scarf instead of letting it blow about her face like that of a wild woman, she should have checked her make-up to make sure that her lipstick was intact and that her nose wasn't shiny. And then she caught herself up short—her aunts would be happy to see her no matter how she looked, and what did she care about impressing Chad Smith, anyway?

The rickety dock—why hadn't it been replaced?—hove into view, and with a surge of joy Paige recognised Aunt Biz and Aunt Sophie hurrying down the steep winding path from the Manse, Aunt Biz tall and spare and moving with slow deliberation, and Aunt Sophie plump as ever, drying her hands on her apron and looking distracted as usual.

Chad slowed the boat and edged it up to the dock, turning off the motor and securing the boat with swift efficiency. Paige, not caring about her suit any more, scrambled out of the boat and was enveloped by the aunts.

When they had released her, they stood back and looked at her. 'But you're so pretty!' exclaimed Aunt Sophie. 'Just like dear Elisabeth at your age. Don't you think so, Biz?'

Aunt Biz held her at arm's length and studied her calmly. 'A bit taller than Elisabeth, perhaps, but the same dark brown hair with a hint of red. And those eyes—no, Elisabeth's eyes were never sea green like yours, Paige. And your face is more oval. Still, you're very much like her. Always were.'

With this observation, Aunt Biz bent to pick up Paige's larger suitcase.

'Oh no, Aunt Biz, I don't want you to carry that,' protested Paige.

'I carry all luggage around here,' said Chad, insistently tugging at the big suitcase until Aunt Biz released it. He hoisted the smaller one too, then stood back, waiting for them to lead.

'You see, he takes such good care of us,' said Aunt Sophie, looking earnestly up at Paige. Aunt Biz just smiled and led the way up the path of crushed oyster shells, evidently agreeing.

Paige, with an uncertain look at Chad, who grinned and waggled his eyebrows at her, turned and followed the aunts, increasingly conscious of Chad's eyes on her slender and shapely legs as she preceded him towards the Manse.

She desperately wanted the Manse to look as she remembered it, and she wasn't disappointed, not much anyway. The Manse was constructed of tabby, a material impervious to time and unique to the area. On the old plantations like St Albans, tabby had been manufactured from a mixture of oyster shells, sand and lime, which was poured into wooden forms and left to harden into a kind of mortar. The Manse, a prime example of tabby construction, was built on a high basement so that the front door must be reached by climbing a graceful flight of stairs. Two chimneys surmounted the low hip roof, and the portico was delicately proportioned and supported by white columns.

The Manse's grey tabby exterior appeared much the same as it always had, but the white paint on the portico and porch railing was dirty and crumbling. Without thinking, Paige reached out and touched her forefinger to the paint on the railing; a good-sized hunk of it flaked off and fell among the azalea bushes surrounding the house. She turned and saw Chad watching her, but when the paint chipped away he didn't even have the good grace to seem embarrassed. She shot him a boldly accusatory look and followed the aunts inside.

Inside, the Manse was dingier and dustier than she had remembered. A central hall divided the downstairs into two halves; on the right was a parlour, on the left a dining room. Surely those velvet draperies at the parlour windows had once been a soft shade of green, not grey. And the lacklustre hardwood floor had, in other days, always been polished to a high sheen beneath the priceless Bokhara rugs.

But the aunts seemed not to notice anything amiss about the Manse. 'Chad, please take Paige's suitcases to the bedroom at the back of the house,' said Aunt Biz. And to Paige, 'We've given you your old room back.'

This, at least, was good news. Paige had always loved

the room the aunts had designated hers so long ago when she used to spend summers at St Albans with her mother. It was a long room, and one wall was composed almost entirely of French doors which led out on to a narrow balcony overlooking the tops of trees with the sea rippling out beyond.

Chad disappeared up the stairs with her luggage, while Aunt Sophie bustled off towards the kitchen to check on dinner.

Aunt Biz settled down on the opposite end of the couch from Paige and folded her hands in her lap. 'So,' she said, her plain face radiating welcome, 'you're here.'

'Yes,' said Paige warmly, reaching over and patting Aunt Biz's hand, 'I'm here. And it's been much too long. I never meant to stay away so long, you know.'

'Well, I know how it is with young people, especially you with your flight schedule. Here one day, gone the next. I must say that working for the airline sounds exciting.'

This seemed to be an ideal time to take Aunt Biz into her confidence, to pour out her heart about the decision she knew she had to make before returning to New York.

'Oh, Aunt Biz,' she began in a rush, 'working for the airline *is* exciting when it affords the chance of meeting someone like Stephen McCall.' Here she paused; her aunt's eyebrows lifted in interest. 'He's a pilot,' Paige went on, more uncertainly now. 'I've dated him for a few months.' As she became increasingly unsure of her aunt's reaction to what she was about to reveal, her words dwindled away at the end of the sentence. She had begun to have serious misgivings about discussing Stephen's demands with either aunt.

She had thought, perhaps unrealistically, that she'd be able to use the aunts as uncritical sounding boards in order to think things through about Stephen in a more realistic way. Yet now, confronted with the chance to talk about him, with Aunt Biz regarding her so expectantly, her head cocked to the side like an alert sparrow, Paige saw just how ridiculous that idea was. How could she ever have thought that she'd be able to get sound advice from two elderly maiden ladies about whether or not to set up unmarried housekeeping with affable, handsome, don't-tie-me-down Stephen McCall?

'So you have a young man! How nice, dear. I'd like to meet him.' Aunt Biz looked at Paige more sharply, sensing Paige's inner agitation, which had increased all the more at her aunt's archaic manner of referring to Stephen. Paige had never before realised how far from the modern world and its modern problems her aunts really lived.

Aunt Biz's brown eyes twinkled at a sudden thought. 'You haven't come to tell us that there's a wedding in the offing, have you, dear?'

Paige felt the colour rush to her face. She shook her head ruefully. 'No . . . no, I most certainly didn't come to tell you *that*,' she said, but the irony in her voice seemed lost on Aunt Biz, who had a faraway expression on her face as she said, 'I remember when Elisabeth, your mother, was married here at the Manse. We strung Japanese lanterns up on the veranda and——'

Aunt Biz's reverie gave Paige the chance to escape on a reverie of her own. Stephen, altogether personable, black-haired and blue-eyed, a devil-may-care Irishman, was pleasant to be with and clearly enamoured of her. But, much to Paige's dismay, even though she liked Stephen, their relationship was lacking that certain something that she had always expected to share with the man she loved. Try as she might, as fond as she was of Stephen, she couldn't manufacture any feelings for him beyond simple affection. It was useless to try.

As for moving in with him, she had reluctantly promised him, against her better judgment, to consider it.

His blue eyes had sparkled winsomely at her when he had broached the subject a few weeks ago over a dinner cunningly complete with candlelight and wine. 'Just think of living together as one of the many alternatives open to us,' he had urged.

Many alternatives? Well, so was marriage an alternative, but he had never mentioned *that*. Paige knew, at this point, that it was either move in with him or lose him entirely—Stephen took pride in not being the marrying kind. She was well aware that other women considered him a good catch and that many would jump at the arrangement he was offering her. Furthermore, he knew how attractive he was to women, and he seemed supremely confident that she would say yes.

She had hoped she would be able to put the whole problem of what to do about Stephen in perspective while she was here, far away from him on St Albans Island. It was going to take some serious thought, because Paige had never been intimate with any man, and setting aside her scruples for Stephen didn't feel right in the place where it mattered most, her heart.

Finally, noticing how Paige was staring off into space, Aunt Biz stopped talking about weddings and said understandingly, 'Well, I suppose you're not ready to give up the freedom you enjoy working for the airline.'

Paige had not yet replied to this when they heard footsteps on the stairs. Aunt Biz turned towards the doorway. 'Ah, here's Chad,' she said with pleasure. 'Won't you join us for a glass of sherry before dinner?'

'No, I don't think so. I need to change my clothes. But what's this I heard about working for an airline?' He turned to Paige and lounged against the doorframe. There was no doubt about it—Chad radiated an aura of raw sexuality. It was evident in the angle at which he held his head, the tilt of his torso, the tight fit of his jeans. 'Is that what you do?'

Paige fought to retain control of her poise. She didn't want him to see the overwhelming effect he had on her, nor did she want her aunt to recognise it, either. 'Yes,' she blurted out finally. 'I'm a flight attendant.'

'And where are you based?'

'New York City. I work on overseas flights—Paris to New York, New York to Brussels.'

'I see. You speak French?'

Paige met his eyes levelly, beginning to feel she had conquered her treacherous senses. 'Yes, fluently.' Too late, she realised that his piercing eyes recalled her unbidden reponse to his kiss on the dock earlier. Quickly her eyes dropped, but not soon enough to avoid seeing the amused self-confidence in his. Damn him, she thought. He knows his effect on women; he's playing with me as a cat plays with a mouse.

'Paige majored in French in college,' added Aunt Biz, oblivious to the seductive interaction between them. Chad continued to watch Paige, his eyes intense, and she wished, not for the first time, that his gaze didn't make her feel so uncomfortable.

Chad lazily removed his shoulder from the doorframe and stretched, showing his long, lean muscles to advantage. He smiled and winked at Aunt Biz. Oh, he was a charmer all right. He probably charmed the snakes out from under their rocks—in addition to little old ladies. He obviously expected Paige, as well, to fall swooning at his feet. And that was one thing, despite his undeniable attractiveness, that she would not do.

'I'll be going now,' he said, putting his hand on the doorknob. 'That is, unless you can think of anything else you need me for.'

'No, no, you've been quite helpful already,' said Aunt Biz, waving him away.

'Fine,' he said. 'See you later.' They could hear him whistling as his feet crunched away along the oyster-shell path.

Paige was just about to blurt out, 'Who *is* he, anyway?' when Aunt Biz, watching him through the deeply recessed window behind them, said fervently,

'Thank goodness for Chad. I don't know what we'd do without him.'

In the face of this unabashed enthusiasm for the handyman's presence on St Albans, Paige prudently decided to hold her tongue. Fortunately Aunt Sophie chose that moment to arrive with three glasses of sherry.

It was an evening ritual at the Manse that Paige well remembered, this gathering in the parlour for dry sherry before dinner. She recalled her mother and her aunts and Uncle John participating in it when she was growing up, and she herself had tasted her first glass of alcoholic beverage here. And in the summer before college, she had been included in the ceremony as an equal, and it was then that she'd first felt completely grown up.

A sense of peace settled over her, and Paige realised suddenly how very much it meant to her to be back on St Albans Island, staying at the Manse, her family's ancestral home, with the aunts. They were all she had in the world, these two; they were her last remaining direct tie to her roots.

Aunt Sophie sneezed, and Paige looked at her sharply. 'You're not catching a cold, are you, Aunt Sophie?' she asked, full of concern. Aunt Sophie, about to sneeze again, shook her head frantically and dug in her pocket for a handkerchief.

'It's her allergy,' explained Aunt Biz. 'You remember, it always acts up this time of year.'

Paige did remember. Aunt Sophie's allergies to myriad pollens and insects were a hard-to-forget feature of summer on St Albans. Often Aunt Sophie would disappear into her room for days at a time to nurse her runny nose or headache, emerging only to supervise the preparation of dinner and to sneeze helplessly while watching everyone else's activity.

This time Aunt Sophie managed to control her sneezing, finally excusing herself to see to their meal.

After several minutes of chatting and catching up on family gossip, Paige left Aunt Biz and climbed the stairs to her room, where she washed and changed into a softly flowing scooped-neck peasant dress in shades of blue and green, one of Stephen's favourites. It had a wide flounced skirt, and Paige pushed the low neckline off her shoulders; the clear colours made her eyes, which Aunt Biz had called sea green, seem even greener.

Her hair, that was the problem. By letting it flap in the breeze she had allowed it to become coated with sticky salt spray. She found her brush in her handbag and brushed her hair vigorously for several minutes, finally restoring its crispness. Her hair was of medium texture with a slight wave; she pinned one side high above her ear with a gold barrette. A new shade of lipstick, one with a coral cast to it, and she was ready to go down to dinner.

Aunt Biz and Aunt Sophie were already seated at the big dimly lit dining-room table when she arrived. The overhead chandelier was missing three flame-shaped bulbs, and Paige made a mental note to ask Chad Smith to replace them. The food was already in place; evidently the aunts had dispensed with a maid. Curious, and influenced by the thin film of dust on the near-by sideboard, Paige asked, 'Whatever happened to the maids you used to have? You know, they all seemed to be named Pearl.'

Aunt Sophie crinkled her eyes in laughter. 'Oh, there were only Big Pearl and Little Pearl. And I'm afraid they've all moved away.'

Paige remembered the tiny fishing village on the north end of the island. Uncle John had allowed several families to live there, descendants of the slaves that used to work the St Albans cotton plantation. Uncle John had believed that their presence on that remote end of the island discouraged trespassers, and the wives and daughters had provided a steady supply of maids at the Manse.

'Moved away? Where did they go?'

'To the seafood processing plant in Brunswick on the mainland, of course. Better salaries and more convenient living conditions.'

'Oh,' said Paige in surprise. She could scarcely imagine St Albans without the fishermen and their lively families in residence.

She started to remove the white linen napkin from its tarnished silver ring, but Aunt Biz put out a hand and rested it on her wrist. 'Not yet, dear,' she said. 'We're waiting for Chad.'

'Chad?' she echoed blankly.

'Of course. He eats his meals with us,' Aunt Biz told her, as though their handyman's presence at their dining-room table was the most natural thing in the world.

The light was so dim that Paige hadn't even noticed the extra place set across the table from her. She blinked at Aunt Biz, then decided against questioning their inclusion of Chad. After all, she could understand that her aunts were lonely with just the two of them to converse, day after day. Chad probably provided them with a welcome diversion.

And then he was there, slamming the front door (the *front* door?) behind him, walking jauntily into the dining room as though it belonged to him. Aunt Sophie's adoring smile was not lost on Paige, nor was Aunt Biz's obvious delight at Chad's presence. Paige tried to hide her dismay at their clear capitulation. What in the world was going on here? How had Chad's influence become so pervasive in her aunts' lives?

'Sorry I'm late,' he apologised, slipping easily into his chair across from Paige. His eyes rested approvingly on her for a moment, taking in the way her dress clung to her rounded breasts. 'My, you look spiffy tonight,' he observed, favouring her with a smile.

Spiffy? She flushed, compressed her lips and narrowed her eyes into green slits, hoping he got the message: *I don't trust you, Chad Smith.* If he did, he didn't show it. Instead, upon Aunt Sophie's urging, he helped himself to a generous portion of squash casserole and an even bigger helping of country-fried steak.

'I can see why you wanted to visit St Albans,' said Chad, addressing her. 'Aunt Sophie's cooking is such a treat. I've never tasted squash prepared this way before—delicious!' He took another mouthful.

Paige's eyes joined with his over the fresh flower centrepiece. 'That's not the only reason I came to St Albans,' she said coldly, hoping he understood her meaning.

'Oh, I'm sure,' he said. His eyes were laughing at her, and she fixed him with a meaningful stare before taking another bite. The man was impossible! He knew what she was trying to say, and he was mocking her. Clearly he knew how firmly entrenched he was with the aunts; he was almost daring her to challenge his position. Fuming inwardly, she continued to eat, but the food had lost its taste. Chad's lighthearted banter with the aunts did little to help her mood.

When the dinner was finally over and Chad had excused himself, Paige helped carry plates and dishes into the Manse's spacious kitchen with the full intention of helping with the clean-up. But Aunt Biz and Aunt Sophie were so determined that she leave it all to them that finally she gave in.

'We know you must be tired after your trip, dear,' Aunt Biz insisted warmly. 'And we like working in the kitchen together, we really do. Let us handle the evening meals, but we're each on our own · for breakfasts, okay?'

Paige goodnaturedly let them push her out of the kitchen and wandered delightedly through the house, renewing her happy acquaintance with all the old things she remembered so well from her childhood summers. The big walnut grandfather clock on the landing, its

brass pendulum swaying slowly back and forth, its
chime still clear. The round gilt mirror in the hall,
reflecting the once well-polished banister and newel
post of the stairway. The tiny brass cat, tarnished now,
that had sat, its tail curled around its front paws, on the
rosewood desk since the aunts were little girls.

Reminiscing, she wandered through the study,
located in the back of the parlour, and flung open the
French doors to the veranda. The floor of the balcony
above, the one outside her room, cast the study in
shadows, but in the distance she could hear the steady
rush of waves to the shore. It didn't take her long to
decide that what she needed to clear her head after a
long, trying day was a swift walk on the beach.

The Manse occupied a rise of land sloping gently to
white sand. Page walked slowly down the slope,
watching her shadow precede her. The moon was full
tonight and shed its light over St Albans, tipping the
crests of the waves in gilt.

When she reached the wide beach, she slipped her
feet out of her shoes and left them hidden in a clump of
sea oats at the dune line. The sand crunched beneath
her toes as she ran swiftly to the edge of the ocean,
stopping just short of the high water mark.

She turned northward and walked beside the sea,
throwing her head back and inhaling deeply. The
fragrance of the Golden Isles was like no other, a heady
blend of sea and sun and marshland, wafted overhead
by the gentlest of breezes. She could feel herself
unwinding, relaxing, becoming one with the island. She
wondered again why she had stayed away so long. Four
years of college in California and her subsequent swift
entry into her present jet-hopping life weren't really
adequate excuses for depriving herself of the pleasures
of St Albans.

With a start she saw a figure walking quickly towards
her along the beach. For a moment she was frightened;
it was unusual to meet another person in this private

place. Then she realised with a sinking feeling that it could be no one but Chad Smith.

She didn't know if he'd seen her or not, but she whirled quickly and began to retrace her footsteps along the shore. She would go back to the house, wash her hair, retire for the evening. She most certainly did not want to encounter him again tonight—dinner with him had been enough of an ordeal.

But Chad apparently didn't feel the same way. 'Paige,' he called. 'Wait for me!'

Paige ignored this, planting one foot in front of the other with absorbed determination. She was almost running, and it must be obvious that she didn't want to talk to him.

He persisted nevertheless. 'Paige! Wait!'

She didn't turn to measure his progress; it seemed best not to acknowledge him at all. She pretended not to notice him when he jogged up behind her.

'My, you make it difficult,' he observed, falling into step.

She shot him an aloof look and continued walking. That one look, however, meant to distance herself from him mentally if not physically, was enough to shoot a feeling of dismay through her. If only he didn't look so irresistibly handsome in the bright moonlight; if only his eyes didn't penetrate her usual reserve and incite her body to respond in the most insane manner!

'I'm delighted to find you out walking tonight,' he went on. 'A walk in the moonlight with you is preferable to the way I usually spend my evenings.'

'And how is that?' she couldn't resist asking. St Albans was hardly what she would have thought a stimulating environment for a bachelor like Chad.

Chad looked down at her, his expression slightly guarded. 'Alone,' he said, and even though Paige's curiosity about how Chad spent his time was not really satisfied, he effectively switched topics.

'You know,' he said smoothly, his tone conversational, 'I've often thought that St Albans had everything I needed—sun, sand, sea, good company, fine food—except a beautiful woman. And now circumstances have even provided that.'

She knew that he was looking down at her with that infuriating grin of his. 'Stop making jokes,' she said in the frostiest tone she could muster, sounding rather the way she sounded when drunks began harassing her in mid-flight. 'I'm not in the mood.'

'Ah,' he said, and she felt his upper arm brush her shoulder—she didn't know if it was by chance or design. 'What *are* you in the mood for?'

She dared a quick glance, but nevertheless it lasted long enough to tell her that his blond hair captured the moonlight in a halo effect and that his amber eyes were warm as they rested upon her face. She deliberately turned her eyes to the ocean, willing herself to ignore him.

Realising that she wasn't about to reply, he continued. 'I see. You're in the mood for what I'm in the mood for. And who wouldn't be?' He waved his arm at the surrounding scenery. 'Moonlight. Ocean. And we're alone, except for each other.'

Paige stopped walking altogether. She could feel her heart speeding up, pulsating in a rhythm, the rhythm of the sea. The rising beat threatened to engulf her, to distract her from her good intentions. 'Listen, Chad Smith, I'm getting tired of your hints. Go away. Can't you see that I——' She spoke frantically, trying to rid herself of him before it was too late.

He turned to face her, planting his feet far apart in the soft sand. He spoke slowly, huskily, but with conscious deliberation. 'I see what I want to see, a beautiful woman with flowing dark hair and eyes the colour of the sea. And I sense that she wants to kiss me almost as much as I want to kiss her.'

Amazed to the point of silence, Paige watched in utter disbelief as he reached out his hands, placed them firmly on her shoulders, and drew her close to him. The strong angular planes of his face stood out in the glow of the moonlight, his eyes seemed lit with an amber fire. Slowly, slowly, Chad gathered her into his arms, and she reacted with a kind of stunned breathlessness. She found herself unable to move; she only stared up at him, moist lips slightly parted, wondering why she found it so difficult to breathe.

Her hair, teased by the soft breeze, blew forward and trailed wispily across his cheek. He noticed it and smiled, but he didn't brush it away. Instead he lowered his head even more so that his lips were all but touching hers. She found herself anticipating his kiss in dismayed wonder, feeling his soft breath on her mouth, the tensing of his muscles as he pressed her unresisting body to his.

And then his knowing lips brushed hers, gently at first, then gradually, more masterfully. Paige felt swept away on a tide of sensation, an emotional surge that bore her away from any vestige of restraint. Her body responded helplessly to the onslaught of his kisses, and he was kissing her again and again. She felt her arms sliding around him, thrilling to the flexing of the muscles in his broad back as he glided his hand upward to wind it in her hair.

Paige had never been kissed like this, not by Stephen, not by anyone else; had never been so aware of her own curves fitting those of a man's body, nor of the sensitive throb of her swelling breasts where they were crushed against his chest. When at last his searching, seeking mouth, so coaxing and so powerfully insistent, released her lips, she gasped, then pushed him away, only to clutch helplessly at his shirt when her knees nearly gave way.

Chad looked down at her shrewdly, and she was aghast to read the amusement in his eyes. 'Well,' he said, 'I suppose you've had enough for tonight. But this is just for openers. I can promise you even more excitement next time.'

She struggled for control of herself and took one small step backward. 'There won't be a next time,' she said, sounding even less sure of her words than she felt.

Chad nodded and turned to walk away from her. He took a few steps down the beach before he tossed over his shoulder, 'Oh, yes, there will. You can count on it,' and then, laughing softly, he hurried away, his tall figure washed in moonlight.

Paige stood, little wavelets lapping at her bare feet, and watched him until he was out of sight. Then, raising one hand to her bruised lips, quelling the primitive desire that had run rampant through her body, she murmured to herself, 'Who *are* you, Chad Smith? Who are you, anyway?'

CHAPTER TWO

'BLACKBERRY jam or muscadine jelly?' asked Aunt Biz, popping a piece of toast out of the toaster.

'Blackberry now, muscadine later,' said Paige, knowing that the aunts made all their own jams and jellies from fruits native to St Albans and that either would be delicious.

Aunt Biz handed Paige her toast and the jar of jam before sitting down across from her at the big round oak kitchen table. 'I hope you don't mind that breakfast is such an informal affair,' said Aunt Biz. 'Sophie likes to sleep late, sometimes until ten or eleven o'clock, and I prefer a quick morning meal so that I can work in my garden before the sun gets too hot. And without a maid——' Aunt Biz shrugged apologetically.

'Why don't you find another maid?' suggested Paige. 'This is such a big house for the two of you to keep up.' She didn't mention the obvious coat of dust over everything, or the tarnished silver and brass, or the floors that needed waxing.

'There isn't anyone,' said her aunt.

'Surely you could find a girl who would be willing to come over from the mainland, perhaps a live-in,' said Paige. 'You could have Chad take her back to Brunswick for the weekends if she preferred.'

Aunt Biz furrowed her brow. 'None of the maids want to live so far away from town. It's not exciting enough here for them. If they get bored, they can't exactly run out to see a movie, you know. No, I'm afraid it's out of the question.'

'I hope you won't mind if I pitch in and help you and Aunt Sophie with the house while I'm here,' said Paige, trying to be tactful. Secretly she couldn't wait to get her hands on a dustcloth.

'Oh, but this is your vacation,' objected Aunt Biz. 'We want you to enjoy yourself.'

'There's nothing that would please me more than helping you take care of these fine old things,' insisted Paige with enthusiasm. 'I live in a tiny apartment in the city, and everything I own is jarringly modern. I'd love working around the Manse if you'll let me.'

'Only if you promise to leave plenty of time for swimming and sunbathing and some of the other things you like to do.'

'I promise,' said Paige, smiling at her aunt. 'And I hope you don't mind if I dig up that old treadle sewing machine. I'd like to make some bright pillows for the couch in the study while I'm here. I enjoy sewing, but I seldom make time for it.'

'Goodness, if you think you can use that old relic, go right ahead. It's in the closet next to your room, and there are thread and scraps of fabric in the closet, too.'

Paige looked forward to refurbishing, even in a minor way, the tired décor at the Manse. It pained her, for her aunts' sake, to see the place looking so decrepit. She'd found that a bank of pillows in cheerful colours could hide even the most dismally upholstered couch and brighten spirits as well. She had brought her needlepoint with her, a small but colourful picture of a heron in flight that she had designed herself. She often worked on needlepoint when she had a long layover at an airport; it helped pass the time pleasurably and made her feel as though she really wasn't wasting it. If she could complete the almost-finished heron picture while she was at St Albans, she could ask Chad to frame it, and the aunts would have a cheerful picture to hang on the wall of, say, the foyer, which desperately needed a decorating lift.

Then, thinking of Chad, remembering the night before and her unsettling encounter with him on the beach, she said, 'Aunt Biz, there are some things I want to ask you. This Chad Smith——'

'I know, isn't he wonderful?' Aunt Biz beamed across the table at Paige. 'We were lucky to find him.'

'*How* did you find him?'

'It was at the dock at Brunswick. I'd gone over to pick up the mail at the post office, and I had trouble with the boat motor—again. There didn't seem to be anyone else around except him, sitting on a coil of rope, and he came over and offered to help. He fixed the motor, but he asked me how far I had to go with it because he was worried that it would stall or something, and when I told him St Albans he seemed really interested and asked me if I had any work he could do——'

'He *asked* you? I thought you offered him the job.'

'Well, not exactly. I said we had lots of repair work that could be done here, and he was looking for a place to live and——'

'You told me his boat had sprung a leak,' said Paige, bewildered. She folded her hands in front of her, her elbows on the tabletop, and rested her chin on her knuckles, regarding her aunt with troubled eyes.

'Did I? Well, it was something like that,' said Aunt Biz vaguely. 'Anyway, he came home with me and he's been here ever since. We don't have to pay him a salary; he only takes room and board. I don't know what we would have done without him.'

'But Aunt Biz,' said Paige patiently, thinking of the glaring state of disrepair at the Manse, 'exactly what has he done to improve things around here?'

'Oh, there were the plumbing and the locks,' said Aunt Biz, and out of kindness Paige decided not to remind her aunt that both of these episodes had turned into fiascos. 'And then he chased a skunk out of the basement for us. And he's very good with the boat motor. And he's been fixing up the Sea House—it looks lovely now.'

Paige felt a quickening of interest. The Sea House had always been one of her favourite places on St Albans. Once used as a guest house when previous generations entertained, it was built of the round ballast stones from ships that had long ago plied the ocean between Europe and the Golden Isles. It nestled amid the tall pale green spears of sea oats behind the dune line on a slight promontory that extended into the Atlantic Ocean. The view from its windows was magnificent with the sea on three sides, and in the old days Paige had often taken her sketchbook there at times when she particularly wanted to be alone. Because no one had used it for years, the Sea House had been allowed to become more and more run-down. She was glad to hear that something had been done to restore it.

'What has he done to the Sea House?' she wanted to know.

Aunt Biz seemed unsure. 'He may have done some carpentry work,' she hedged. 'And he's taken a lot of things down there, a table, for instance.'

'Don't you *know* what he's doing? After all, it's your property.' Her voice sounded sharper than she had intended, and instantly she regretted her harsh tone. It was just that she felt so perplexed, so unnerved, at this stranger's involvement in her aunts' lives. She couldn't bear to think that these two elderly ladies, so dear to her, might have fallen under the influence of someone who could very well turn out to be unscrupulous.

'I've only been inside once or twice,' said Aunt Biz, defending herself, and Paige was amazed. Aunt Biz had always insisted on a hands-on approach to running St Albans Island, personally making every decision that affected the island, the Manse, or their inhabitants. In the past she would never have turned over an important project such as rehabilitating the Sea House to a stranger. She would have been there supervising, giving orders, and probably wielding a hammer herself.

For the first time Paige admitted to herself that the

aunts were getting old. They didn't have the vigour to take care of things the way they used to. After all, they were both well into their seventies, and Aunt Biz was the elder by three or four years. A slowing down was to be expected.

'Anyway,' Aunt Biz went on, oblivious to Paige's uneasiness, 'why don't you take Chad's breakfast down to him? I'm sure he'd be happy to show you what he's done to the Sea House.'

'You—you mean he *lives* there?' Paige had thought he must be occupying one of the compact servants' rooms in the Manse's basement; it had never occurred to her that he might be installed in the Sea House.

'Why, of course. Where else would he live?' Aunt Biz was looking at her as though she doubted Paige's good sense.

'I had thought—I mean, the basement——'

'We couldn't very well let him live there, dear, especially after the skunk.'

'I—I see,' said Paige, not really seeing at all.

Aunt Biz rose from the table and went to the sink where she ran water over her dishes and sudsed them quickly. 'I want to get out in the garden, so . . .'

'You go right ahead,' said Paige, getting up and putting a slender arm around Aunt Biz's shoulders. For the first time, she realised that Aunt Biz seemed smaller, stooped. Aunt Biz had always been so robust and so hearty. For a moment Paige felt a great surge of tenderness towards her aunts. If only she had realised sooner, she would have visited long before this—long before Chad Smith ever came on the scene to complicate matters. In fact, if she had come to St Albans earlier, maybe her aunts never would have needed him at all. She felt a quick pang of regret. Well, there was nothing she could do now except try to solve their problems as best she could. And she would, as soon as she figured out what was going on here.

Aunt Biz might be slightly more frail than she had

ever been, but there was nothing fragile about her spirit. She paused as she pulled on her old gardening smock and the floppy straw hat that protected her skin from the sun. 'Now if you decide to take Chad his breakfast, he likes a soft-cooked egg in one of those little cups from the top shelf of the cupboard and an English muffin with——'

'I think I'll let Chad Smith cook his own meal,' said Paige tightly. If the aunts enjoyed catering to their handyman, that was one thing, but she had no intention of waiting on him, even to see the Sea House. She carried her own breakfast dishes to the sink and began to wash them, trying not to show Aunt Biz her agitation at the very idea of becoming Chad Smith's resident cook.

'Well, all right, if you don't feel like cooking,' said Aunt Biz uncertainly, and then as she glanced out the door her expression brightened. 'It looks like he's on his way over here to do just that.' She hurried out the back door and exchanged greetings with Chad before disappearing down the path towards her garden plot.

'Good morning, merry sunshine,' said Chad brightly when he saw Paige glowering at him from her place at the sink. 'What makes you look so cheerful this morning?' He opened the refrigerator door and removed an egg. 'Care for an egg? I understand you turned down the opportunity to cook my breakfast, but I don't mind cooking yours.'

'No, thanks,' said Paige. 'I've eaten.'

Chad closed the refrigerator door and found a pan in the cupboard. He filled it with water, placed it on the stove burner, and began to prepare his egg, whistling through his teeth. He seemed in fine fettle this morning, on top of his world and all that was in it. Well, why shouldn't he be? To even the most casual onlooker, it would be clear that Chad Smith was in control on St Albans.

Paige continued to dry her dishes, but Chad's aimless

whistling began to grate on her nerves. 'Would you please stop that!' she burst out finally.

'Stop fixing my breakfast? Surely you jest. Why, Aunt Biz and Aunt Sophie allow me full run of the Manse, including the kitchen. And since you didn't want to prepare my meal, what choice do I have? Would you rather I go hungry? I doubt——'

'I'm not talking about your breakfast and you know it!' exploded Paige, throwing her dishtowel down on the floor. 'It's that awful whistling of yours that I can't stand.'

Chad stood regarding her with one raised eyebrow, arms crossed across his chest. His face looked freshly shaven and she caught a whiff of his aftershave lotion, a pungent outdoorsy scent. 'Temper, temper,' he said, bending with an athletic grace to pick up her dishtowel. 'I wouldn't go throwing things around like that. The aunts like to keep everything shipshape around here, you know.'

'That's exactly what I want to talk to you about,' she retorted hotly, but Chad looked at his watch. It was a slim quartz model, Paige noticed, probably gold and obviously expensive. Again, his watch didn't fit his handyman image.

'Sorry, but our talk will have to wait until after I eat my egg,' he told her, turning away to take the egg from the water with a slotted spoon. He deposited it carefully in an eggcup leaned back against the counter, holding the cup in his hand and dipping into the egg with a spoon. 'Delicious. The secret is to let it boil exactly four minutes—no more, no less. You'll have to let me cook you one some time.'

'You are the most infuriating man,' she commented, watching him eat the egg with exasperation.

'Because I eat four-minute eggs? Really, that shows an uncommon sort of prejudice. I wouldn't have thought it of you.' He eyed her brief costume of flared lavender shorts paired with a back-buttoned cap-sleeved blouse in hot pink. 'Now it happens that I have a prejudice too. I just can't stand the colour combination of pink and purple. It brings out the worst in me, especially when worn by a gorgeous brunette.' He set aside the eggcup and bent over and kissed her quickly on the cheek. 'You see? It brings out the worst.'

Paige retreated to the opposite side of the kitchen. 'I don't know what you're up to, Chad Smith, but you'd better stop it. You may have my aunts buffaloed, but you'll have a hard time getting around me.'

Chad fished his English muffin out of the toaster and sent her a calculating look. 'I can see that, all right. You're bound and determined to make it difficult. I'll just have to win you over, that's all.'

'And exactly how will you do that?'

'Oh, leave it to me. You can't expect me to outline my plan of action to the enemy, can you?'

'I suppose not,' she said, wishing she'd never become involved in this exchange. And although the talk resembled goodnatured joshing, she sensed an underlying seriousness behind Chad's words. He was letting her know that he wasn't to be run off so easily.

'Of course, I read somewhere that in order to rid yourself of an enemy, you must make him your friend. Do you suppose, in your case, that it's possible?' He finished off the muffin nonchalantly, but she sensed that he was waiting for her answer.

'Possible? Yes. Likely? No.' She tried her best to look indifferent, which wasn't easy. Chad called up a number of reactions on her part, and indifference, sorry to say, wasn't one of them.

Chad washed his dishes with quick efficiency and dried his hands on a paper towel. Paige couldn't help noticing how strong they were, with capable squared-off fingers, broad calloused palms, and wide sinewy wrists.

'Now, I believe you wanted to talk to me,' and he stood, hands on his hips, regarding her with a challenge in his eyes. 'It had something to do with keeping things shipshape, as I recall.'

Paige closed her eyes and drew a deep breath. When she opened them again, she saw that Chad was looking at her with that unfathomable concentration of his, a deep piercing look that seemed to plunge beneath the surface to grasp her very soul. She turned her back to him so he couldn't see his effect on her and walked briskly across the room to the pantry. She had made up her mind not to let his intense masculinity rattle her.

'As you're the handyman, I think you need to take more responsibility for the Manse and its upkeep,' she said. She opened the pantry door and rummaged on the shelf where she knew the aunts kept a supply of light bulbs. She found several of the flame-shaped variety used in the dining room chandelier and held them out to Chad. 'Last night I noticed that three bulbs in the dining-room chandelier need replacing. They should be replaced immediately.'

'Well,' he said reluctantly, 'all right. I'll need a ladder.'

'I'm sure you can find one.'

His eyes locked with hers, not giving an inch. He might get the ladder, he might change the bulbs, but he would in no way let Paige be in charge, and she knew it. 'There's a ladder in the basement,' he said; then he wheeled and disappeared out the back door.

Paige waited for Chad in the dining room, wishing that she felt free to complain to the aunts about him, but how could she when they clearly doted on him?

It was certainly a sticky situation. And after all, maybe having Chad Smith around wasn't all bad. As Aunt Biz had pointed out, most people didn't want to live on isolated St Albans, and at least he'd be there to help if there were ever an emergency. She shuddered to think about the aunts alone during a storm or the possibility that one or both of them might fall ill. She gritted her teeth and made up her mind to tread lightly, at least at first.

But he was certainly taking his time finding that ladder, Paige thought, glancing restlessly at her wristwatch. When finally he did show up, he dawdled at pulling aside the huge dining-room table and stalled at setting the ladder up beneath the chandelier which, because of the twelve-foot-high ceilings of the Manse, was uncommonly high.

Paige watched him wrestle with the ladder for a few minutes before she exclaimed impatiently, 'Chad, anyone would think you've never seen a ladder before in your life! I'm beginning to think I should have done this myself!'

He ignored her and climbed to the top, swaying awkwardly as he reached down for the bulbs. She watched him as he replaced the old bulbs, thinking how incongruous he looked at the top of the ladder, how ill at ease he seemed with this whole chore.

When he had clambered down the ladder in obvious relief, and Paige had tried the light switch to make sure the new bulbs were functioning, he said, 'I'll put this ladder away and be right back.'

After he had gone, Paige found a pencil and paper in a drawer and headed her list WORK TO DO. She had decided to make a list of chores that needed to be done on St Albans; while she was here she would check them off as Chad completed them. Maybe all he needed to turn him into a useful employee was a bit of organisation, a certain amount of direction. And she, rather than the aunts, seemed to be the one to supply it.

First on the list was PAINT OUTSIDE WOOD TRIM, and she was just starting to write PAINT KITCHEN when Chad strode whistling up the back steps.

'What's that?' he asked, leaning down over her shoulders and resting his broad hands on the table on both sides of her. The insides of his arms pressed lightly against the outsides of hers; with anyone else, the touch wouldn't be suggestive, but with Chad Smith it most definitely was. She felt his warm breath on the back of her head. It was a mesmerising feeling, being so near to him, and she was glad that she couldn't see his face. She'd done well at keeping her distance from him this morning, both physically and emotionally, and she intended to persevere in her determination not to let him capture any part of her suddenly unsteady emotions.

'I'm working on a list of things for you to do,' she said meaningfully, shrinking from his touch.

He remained where he was, bending over her, pretending not to notice her retreat. He scanned the list and whistled. 'Oh, sorry, I keep forgetting that you don't like my whistling. But you don't waste time, do you?'

She summoned her resolve and pushed his arms away. He straightened, walked around the table to face her.

'No, I don't waste time, and you shouldn't either,' she responded pointedly. 'I can't for the life of me think of what you've been doing all day every day since October. The Manse is in a shocking state of disrepair, and I can't imagine why the aunts let you get away with it. I refuse to let you take advantage of them.'

Chad's eyes hardened and he looked as though he were about to say something, but apparently he thought better of it. He turned away from her and said lightly, 'Never would I take advantage of two lovely ladies like Aunt Sophie and Aunt Biz. Now *you* I might take advantage of.'

For a moment she had almost believed in his sincerity when he had said he wouldn't take advantage of the aunts, but he had ruined the effect of his words when he added that bit about taking advantage of her. Well, she was determined that he wouldn't take advantage of anyone around here. Including her.

She pushed her chair away from the table. 'Look, don't you have some work you could be doing?'

He looked down at her through sand-coloured lashes. 'Indeed I do. A special request from Aunt Biz, and I assured her I'd get to it this morning. Trouble is, she said I should take you along with me. Said you know all the good places to go.' His gaze was easy, casual.

'Good places for what?' Paige tried to sound briskly impersonal.

'Crabbing, of course. And I said that was obvious, since you seemed to be so crabby yourself. Will you go with me? Aunt Biz said you would.' He smiled at her appealingly.

'I am not crabby,' she began, but when she saw the teasing merriment in his eyes she couldn't go on. Of course she had been out of sorts ever since she'd met him. And like it or not, they were going to have to co-exist on this small island while she decided what to do about him.

'All right,' she said, taking a deep breath, 'I'll go.'

'Great!' said Chad, looking jubilant. 'The aunts have planned a big party for tonight in honour of your presence—on the beach, with a bonfire. We're going to cook the crabs then.'

'A party? But who would come to a party?'

'Why, you and me and the aunts, of course. Don't spoil it for them. They've been planning it for days. I've hauled so much driftwood for the fire that I've nearly strained my sacro-iliac. You have no choice—we're having that party. But first we capture the crabs.'

Paige remembered with a touch of nostalgia how she used to go crabbing in the quiet saltwater marshes of St Albans with the children of the fishermen who used to live here. She had always loved poking through the marsh grass, looking for a likely spot, then dropping the bait and waiting for a crab to take it. She had never even minded tying the bait—fish heads or chicken necks—on the lines.

She put aside her list of chores and followed Chad down the path to the shed at the edge of the forest.

Here beneath the swaying grey beards of Spanish moss hanging from the live oak trees they paused while Chad opened the shed and rummaged around for two crabbing nets and the bait.

'Did the aunts tell you that they no longer have to walk wherever they want to go on St Albans? They travel first class these days,' said Chad. Paige followed him around the back of the shed where a lean-to had been constructed. It sheltered a white golf cart with a fringed red-and-white canvas top.

'When did they get this?' asked Paige, charmed. Getting around St Albans on a series of rutted paths had always been something of a problem, and she knew that walking the distances involved could be difficult for the aunts at their age.

'A few months ago,' said Chad. 'Let's get in and you can direct me to the best crabbing places.'

Paige remembered a tiny salt-water creek near the fishermen's settlement on the north end of the island, so she told Chad how to get there and settled back on the cushioned seat to enjoy the ride. And she might as well enjoy it, she reflected. After all, there she was on St Albans, her own particular version of paradise, in the company of a very virile man who was undeniably attractive. It was up to her to keep her emotions in check, and suddenly she felt equal to the task. She raised her chin and shot Chad a totally unexpected smile. He reacted with a surprised look and seemed to relax. He smiled too, mostly to himself, but it was a good omen, Paige thought. At least, for once, he wasn't making a pass at her. And Stephen McCall had never been further from her mind.

The golf cart hummed over the woodland path, taking in stride broken bits of shell and gnarled tree roots.

'The aunts remember how their father rode an old mule around the island,' said Chad, 'so they've nicknamed the golf cart the Mule. I'm afaid the name's going to stick.'

Paige smiled. Aunt Biz and Aunt Sophie seemed to imprint everything on St Albans with their unique personalities.

The path to the north end of the island wound through a forest of red cedars which sheltered them with thick tufts of blue-green foliage. Here and there they saw woody yellow jessamine vines, their five-lobed yellow flowers lending sweet fragrance to the air. Fuzzy black-and-yellow striped bumblebees buzzed among pink honeysuckle blossoms, gathering nectar to take back to the hives near the Manse.

Chad didn't speak, and Paige felt no urge to begin a conversation. She couldn't admit even to herself that she was overpoweringly aware of his presence beside her, of the skilled manner in which he steered the Mule along the tricky path, of the golden hair that covered his tanned arms.

The Mule lurched over an exposed tree root, sending Paige sideways and off balance; he put out his hand to steady her, letting it remain on her knee for a moment too long. Her hip rested lightly against his on the narrow seat. He was a big man, and there was little room left over for her, even though she was petite. The contact of their bodies brought to mind her own unbidden sensations the night before when he kissed her on the beach. She had almost lost control of herself, and that had never happened before. When Chad had kissed her, she had felt strange, dangerous responses, signs of her own sensuality, rising to the surface. Remembering them, embarrassed by them, she edged over to her own side of the seat, willing him not to notice.

But he did notice, she could tell from the way he flicked his eyes towards her and then back again to the path. He chose to ignore the way she had imposed a space between them, though, and she studied him as he concentrated on driving the Mule. His profile was strong, with a fine high brow and a straight well-shaped nose. His lips betrayed a hint of sensuality, the bottom lip fuller than the top, and his chin had a determined set to it with a barely perceptible cleft. All in all, it was a very nice face, patrician rather than plebeian, and certainly not the kind of face you would expect to find on an itinerant handyman.

They reached the edge of the cedar forest and traversed a meadow trail to the bank of the creek. The creek was as Paige had remembered it, bordered by big rose mallow shrubs interspersed with clumps of milkwort, in bloom now with thick heads of orange flowers.

Paige led Chad, who carried the crabbing gear, to the place where the creek emptied into the marsh. There they waded, their feet protected by high boots, into the shallow water. Beyond the mouth of the creek, the water of the marshland shimmered like a hundred thousand sequins cast adrift amid the pale shafts of the tall marsh grass.

'Here,' said Chad, expecting an indignant objection from her as he handed her a line and a chicken neck. She merely smiled and proceeded to tie the chicken neck on the end of the line without a complaint. This earned his respect, and they stood quietly, dangling their lines in the water, waiting for a crab to bite.

They didn't have to wait long. Paige was the first to get a bite at her chicken neck, and she scooped the crab up in her net.

'Look at the size of this one,' she said triumphantly. The crab was a good six inches across; crabs had to measure at least five inches, or it was required by law that they be thrown back. She shook the crab out of her net into the bucket and dropped her bait back in the water.

Today the crabs were hungry, because before long they had a bucketful. Chad carried the bucket back to the golf cart and watched her remove her boots. 'You're good at this,' he told her. 'Aunt Biz was right.'

'Thanks,' she said, surprised at her pleased reaction to his approval. 'I spent my childhood summers here, you know.'

'What was it like growing up on St Albans?' he asked her as he turned the Mule back towards the Manse.

'It was beautiful,' she told him, long-forgotten scenes from her memory flooding her mind. In a rush she found herself telling him about shelling expeditions on the beach just after a hurricane had passed by far out to sea, dredging up shells in all colours, sizes and shapes. She remembered oyster roasts on the beach around big bonfires when they and their guests from the mainland and St Simons sat on thick logs and told supposedly true ghost stories. He smiled along with her when she told him about climbing the spreading live oak trees and gathering huge clumps of Spanish moss to decorate her tree house.

'The tree house looked beautiful,' she remembered ruefully, 'but I didn't. I was rewarded for my efforts by a horrendous case of chiggers, and I felt itchy for days.'

When they arrived at the Manse, she realised that she had been chattering nonstop, and she stopped talking immediately in embarrassment.

'I'm sorry,' she said, abashed. 'I don't know what made me run on like that; maybe it's just that you seemed so interested.'

'Don't apologise,' he said, and his unusually flecked eyes were warm upon her flushed face. 'I am interested—in St Albans. And in you.'

His gaze discomfited her, and she climbed quickly out of the Mule.

'See you tonight,' he said, and then he was driving away, leaving her to stare after him in perplexity. It wasn't at all like her to confide in strangers, yet she had opened her heart to him, sharing all the special memories of her childhood and St Albans that she had never wanted to share with anyone else. And perhaps strangest of all, she still didn't even know anything about him.

CHAPTER THREE

IT had turned into an exceptionally hot afternoon for May, but the heat hadn't stopped Aunt Sophie. She had prepared a corn soufflé, a jellied salad, a tossed salad, and two desserts, a pistachio cake and a vinegar pie.

Paige, who had painstakingly removed several furry layers of dust from the living and dining rooms before taking to the beach for a sunbath, wandered downstairs fresh from her shower. She had decided after much thought that she should wear her white piqué one-piece swimsuit with the matching wrap-around skirt; it was a cool outfit and she could shed the skirt if she decided to go for a swim.

She appeared in the kitchen to find Aunt Sophie busy, if disorganised.

Paige opened the refrigerator, shook the jellied salad to see if it still wiggled, and swiped a bit of pale green frosting from the pistachio cake. 'I came to help, Aunt Sophie,' she announced, only to discover that Aunt Sophie, unfortunately, had seen her licking the pistachio frosting off her finger.

Aunt Sophie sent her an amused but meaningful look. 'I'm not so sure I need that kind of help,' she protested goodnaturedly. 'You'll be poking your finger into the vinegar pie next!'

'Now, Aunt Sophie,' objected Paige, 'I'm a very good cook. After all, you taught me yourself. Remember the time we made blueberry muffins for Aunt Biz's birthday?'

'How well I remember!' exclaimed Aunt Sophie, raising her eyes to the ceiling. 'You put in twice the amount of baking powder they needed, and we had blueberry muffins rising clear out of the oven!'

'You might say they were rising to the occasion,' said Paige with a wry smile at her own pun.

Aunt Sophie laughed and said, 'I think the blueberry muffins were your worst mistake. You've probably learned quite a lot about cooking by this time.'

'I'm pretty good at making grilled cheese sandwiches, and I've even baked a few Alaskas,' Paige told her.

'Unfortunately, grilled cheese sandwiches aren't on tonight's menu, and as for Baked Alaska—well, with my weight problem, I don't dare tempt myself with a third dessert. Here, wrap these potatoes in aluminium foil, if you'd like to help. I need to attend to the soufflé.'

Paige obediently tore strips of aluminium foil and wrapped several large baking potatoes. She and Aunt Sophie worked companionably together, with Paige humming as she worked.

'There! Foiled again,' she said when she had completed the job. She grinned at Aunt Sophie's martyred look at yet another pun. 'Now what?'

Aunt Sophie handed Paige a basket. 'Put the potatoes in here and take them down to Chad on the beach, dear,' she said. 'He's building the bonfire and he needs to nestle these down in the coals so they can bake slowly before we begin boiling the crabs.'

'But I thought I'd help you in the kitchen,' objected Paige. She didn't particularly welcome any activity that would put her in close proximity to Chad.

'Sorry, but you're banished,' insisted Aunt Sophie. 'Two bad puns in a row are more than I can stand!' She smiled and brushed a strand of grey hair from her damp brow before shooing Paige out of the door.

Paige had hoped to take advantage of her time alone with Aunt Sophie in the kitchen to pump her aunt for more information about Chad. But Aunt Sophie's banishment was absolute, and she found herself walking alone down the incline from the Manse.

It was dusk, and the windswept trees bordering the

beach stood out in stark relief against the blue-grey sky. The ocean, calm tonight, rippled softly towards shore, the waves murmuring gently as they spilled across the sand.

Chad stood watching an infant blaze licking at the big pieces of driftwood piled high on the beach. He wore cut-off denim jeans and a white shirt, its crisp collar thrown open at the throat to expose the thick golden mat of hair on his tanned chest. His light hair was ruffled by the mild breeze; one yellow lock slanted across his sun-bronzed forehead. He looked up when he saw her walking barefoot towards him with the willow basket on her arm. The last rays of the sun caught and held the amber in his eyes.

'You're early,' he observed, taking in her white piqué ensemble and her new suntan.

'I know. Aunt Sophie sent me with the potatoes,' she said, holding the basket towards him, almost as though it were a gesture of goodwill. 'She said you'd know what to do with them.'

'Indeed I do, but I'm not ready to put them on the fire yet. Sit down and keep me company while I wait.'

'Well, I——'

'Come on, don't be so standoffish. I won't bite you, you know.' He sat down on a log and motioned for her to join him.

Paige perched stiffly on the log next to him, holding the basket in her lap, watching the bright orange-yellow flames lap at the bleached driftwood. Shaking his head and regarding her with a perceptive grin, Chad reached over and removed the basket. 'You're acting like Little Red Riding Hood about to meet the wolf. You can put this down. You don't need protection from me.'

'My, Grandma, what a big ego you have,' she retorted. 'What makes you think you frighten me?'

'I don't think "frightened" is the correct word to describe your attitude. You do seem very suspicious of me, however.' He was watching her thoughtfully and with, she thought, an alertness overlaid with almost palpable tension.

The conversation was already becoming too personal for her taste. Of course she was suspicious of him; who wouldn't be? He had moved in so smoothly and set himself up so comfortably and spoke so glibly that he might very well be the greatest con artist of all time. But she wasn't ready for a showdown at this point; she needed time to observe, time to learn the true situation on St Albans. And once she determined that nothing was amiss, if nothing truly was, then she would be only too happy to leave St Albans and her aunts in Chad Smith's hands. One thing was certain—she didn't want to be responsible for an ugly scene that would upset her aunts, particularly here and now.

When she didn't speak, he flashed his white teeth at her in a smile that could only be called enigmatic. Unbidden, the words leaped into her head: *Grandma, what big teeth you have.* She didn't say them, much to her credit. But just thinking them made her smile too, and Chad relaxed visibly as he mistakenly thought she was beginning to soften towards him.

Chad stood up and raked the fire into a bed of white-hot coals. Watching him, unavoidably noticing again his intensely masculine good looks, she couldn't help recalling last night's sensual scene on this very spot. She was determined that nothing like it would happen again between her and Chad, despite his promise that there would be more. And what would *that* involve? she wondered. Chad Smith didn't look like the type who could be satisfied with a few kisses. Come to think of it, if last night were any indication, neither would she. And that was as good a reason as any to avoid further involvement.

There was no denying his effect on her, even now as they quietly watched the gently billowing rise and fall of the sea. Chad possessed a quality of strength and energy that Paige had encountered in no one else.

Perhaps it was his predominantly outdoor life that had left its imprint on him, that made him seem more rugged, more individual than other men she knew. Or perhaps it was the kind of life he led, the life of a drifter.

But Chad Smith didn't fit the stereotype of a common drifter, and that was what she found most disturbing about him. Indeed, despite his joking manner, she sensed that Chad possessed a purposefulness, a determination that he had gone to a good deal of trouble to conceal from her. She puzzled this over in her mind.

'I think it's time to put those potatoes on,' said Chad, rising from the log and carefully packing the potatoes into the hot ashes.

When he had rejoined her, Paige decided it was time to venture a question, taking timely advantage of his presumed softening of her attitude. She hoped to catch him off his guard. 'Where did you live before you lived here?' she asked, trying to get just the right note of sociable curiosity into her voice.

Chad shot her a sharp look. 'Oh, various places. Around,' and he waved his arm in a semi-circle.

Paige regarded him silently, staring at his finely chiselled profile, wondering if she should let him off so easily. She had made up her mind to find out something about him, however, and so tenaciously she held on to the topic. 'Close to the ocean? Aunt Biz said you have a boat, so I assume you were near water.'

'Yes, of course,' he said with something resembling relief. But he volunteered no other information.

She tried again. 'What kind of boat is it?'

He hesitated, his reluctance obvious. 'A sailboat,' he said finally.

'I see,' she said. 'There are all kinds of sailboats,' she said after a pregnant pause during which she hoped he might continue the conversation. 'What kind is yours?'

'Hey, why the third degree?' he said impatiently,

fixing her with a forceful glare that all too clearly warned her to back off.

'It's not a third degree, it's called polite interest. I heard that you had a boat and I thought you might want to talk about it, that's all. We should be able to carry on a decent conversation, you know.' Despite her determination to keep cool, she couldn't help bristling a bit.

Chad rose from the log and walked irritably to the edge of the ocean, keeping his back to her. When he finally turned, she could see that he had subdued his defensiveness, though not completely. His voice was smooth, but the remnants of annoyance revealed themselves in his flashing eyes.

'I don't care to talk about my boat,' he said curtly. And then more softly, 'And yes, we should be able to carry on a decent conversation. And we will. But not at the moment, because I see Aunt Biz and Aunt Sophie wending their way through the trees, and they appear laden with goodies. You'd better go give them a hand while I set up the portable table and put on the water for the crabs.'

Thus he dismissed her, leaving her to help the aunts and wondering what hidden nerve she had exposed.

Paige and the aunts set the table and spread out Aunt Sophie's feast. Chad produced a huge pot two-thirds full of water to which he added a generous pinch of salt and a dollop of vinegar. When the water had come to a rolling boil, he dropped in the crabs they had caught earlier and cooked them for several minutes.

They ate dinner sitting on canvas fold-up stools around the big camp table. Eating the crabs was always a more difficult proposition than catching them. Starting from the underside of the crab, they pried up the apron with a sharp knife. Then the top shell could be lifted off and the appendages discarded. When at last they reached the edible portion beneath the semi-transparent membrane, they grasped the crab on each side, broke it in half, and picked out the meat.

Chad's good humour was very much in evidence. He joked with the aunts, prodded Paige with a few witty comments, and supervised the breaking apart of the crabs. Once he got up from his seat and walked deliberately around the table to lean over Paige's shoulder to help her with a particularly stubborn crab claw. She concentrated mightily on blocking out her lightning response to his nearness. Whenever he touched her, she felt a prickle of excitement; it was altogether too embarrassing. He acted as though he hadn't noticed his effect on her, and perhaps he really hadn't. It was impossible to tell, for unlike her, he seemed always to be completely in charge of his emotions.

After they had eaten their fill, Chad added more driftwood so that the fire revived. The four of them sat on the logs around the flickering blaze, watching the golden globe of the moon as it rose and cast its gilt path across the deep blue water. Paige felt luxuriously lazy and too full to move; she slid down into the sand and leaned back against the log, not caring for the moment that the fire was too close and made her face feel hot.

'Paige,' said Aunt Sophie, 'I saw your list. I simply won't have you working so hard while you're at the Manse.'

Paige hadn't forgotten about her ambitious plan for Chad's time; she had thought of several items she could add to the WORK TO DO list since this morning. 'Don't worry,' she said. 'I'm not the one who'll be doing all the work. Chad is.' She took great pleasure in the widening of his eyes across the fire.

'Oh, but dear, you've listed so much painting to be done. Why, it will take months!'

'Perhaps it will,' she said sweetly, almost laughing at the expression on Chad's face. Clearly the idea of spending several months painting and repairing the Manse wasn't at all to his liking. He gave up trying to look neutral and raised an eyebrow in blatant disapproval.

'We'll have to get some colour charts and choose the paint colours for the inside of the Manse,' Paige went on, ignoring Chad, 'and I suppose you'll want the outside trim done in white again.'

'I already have the paint for the kitchen,' said Aunt Biz unexpectedly. 'It's sorted in the basement. I bought it a long time ago when I thought I could get the painters to come out to St Albans; in fact, I hired them, but they never showed up. It would be such a relief to have the job done.'

'Great,' said Paige, plunging on. 'Chad could start painting the kitchen immediately, if you like.'

She almost expected Chad to leap up from his lounging position on the opposite side of the fire and refuse, but with a great effort he held his tongue. Neither Aunt Biz nor Aunt Sophie seemed to notice Chad's out-and-out reluctance to do the work, and Paige congratulated herself. She'd get some work out of him yet!

'Ah-choo!' went Aunt Sophie unhappily.

'Well,' said Aunt Biz, 'it looks as though we've stayed long enough. Sophie, we'd better get you indoors before every bit of pollen on St Albans zooms in for an attack.'

'Don't worry about cleaning up,' said Chad. 'I'll bring everything up to the Manse later. I'm going to stay here until the fire dies down.'

'Paige?' The aunts waited to see if she would walk to the Manse with them.

She shook her head. Suddenly the unseasonable warmth of the day and the heat of the fire on her face had combined to make her feel sticky and out of sorts. 'I'm going for a quick swim—I'll be there in a few minutes.'

When the aunts had gone, Paige lay with her head propped up against the log, her eyes closed. It had been a full day; no wonder she felt tired. Not to mention the mental strain of assessing Chad Smith and trying to figure out the real reason he was here at St Albans.

She felt a slight stirring at her side and sat up straight when she saw that Chad had walked around to her side of the fire and was sitting beside her. The firelight gilded his hair and brows; his skin seemed golden in its glow.

'Don't get up,' he said softly. 'You look lovely with the firelight playing over your face. It makes you look softer somehow, less stern.'

'Stern? Is that the way I appear to you?'

'Sometimes. Often. You don't like me, I know that.' His tone was resigned.

'Like you? I hardly know you,' she said.

'And you'd rather not,' he replied. The long tie to her wrap-around skirt lay on the sand between them; he picked it up and wound it between his fingers. 'Admit it, you wish I'd leave St Albans.'

Paige felt that anything she said might be easily misinterpreted at this point. She delayed answering for a time, watching the plume of grey smoke as it was caught by the wind and wafted inland. Now and then glowing sparks spiralled upward and were quickly extinguished in the breeze.

'Not exactly,' she said carefully, thinking, as she had earlier in the day, that actually she was very relieved that someone lived here with the aunts in case of emergency. Somehow this didn't seem like the proper time to tell Chad that she questioned his motives in being here—his motives and the pretence under which he had inveigled Aunt Biz to invite him to St Albans. Now, at this very moment, she felt she had ample cause to doubt that he was what he said he was. He didn't seem to know the first thing about repairs, and he obviously hated the idea of painting. Their earlier conversation this evening even shed doubt on his claim that he owned a boat.

'Then if you're not entirely sure you want me to go, why must you keep baiting me? That's what you're doing, you know.' His voice was low and resonant over the murmur of the sea and the crackling of the fire.

Paige turned her head so that she looked full into his face. For once there was no mischievous grin on his lips; instead they were slightly parted, and his brow was knitted in earnestness. She noticed tiny lines around his eyes, lines she hadn't noticed before. She tried to concentrate on his question, if only she could remember what it was! If only he wouldn't look at her that way, if only she could overcome the ridiculous impulse to melt into his arms. Oh yes, he wanted to know why she kept baiting him. He had dropped the tie of her skirt and sat perfectly still, waiting for her reply.

'I—I'm just watching out for my aunts,' she said, dismayed that the pitch of her voice sounded high and nervous.

'You think they can't take care of themselves?'

'I realise that they're getting older,' she began, but Chad interrupted her vehemently.

'They are, but don't sell your Aunt Sophie or your Aunt Biz short.'

'I don't think I am,' retorted Paige, and then, tempering her abrupt response, she said more quietly, 'You forget, I haven't seen them in years. They've changed a bit, you know.'

He considered this. 'I suppose they have.'

It was interesting, Paige thought to herself, how quickly Chad had jumped to the aunts' defence. She wouldn't have expected it of him. His championing of them bespoke something good about his character, and quite frankly, it surprised her. She was astonished to find that it even pleased her.

'Anyway, I was going for a swim,' she said, deciding it was high time she put an end to this conversation. She started to get up, but Chad put out a strong hand and rested it on her shoulder.

'Not yet,' he said quietly. 'Last night I promised you that there'd be a next time. And,' he added, his voice low and melodious, 'I never, never break a promise.'

He slid his hand from her shoulder down the inside of her arm, slowly, taking his time, and his hand gripped hers firmly. Paige could feel the calluses on his palm and wondered briefly what kind of work he had done to get them. His grip was strong and she tried to pull her hand away, but his fingers tightened and refused to release hers.

She twisted her head to look at him, so handsome in the firelight, and his eyes caught and held hers prisoner. His nostrils flared as he leaned forward on his free arm, bringing his face within inches of hers. Then, suddenly, both arms were around her, holding her delicately, savouring the heat of her soft flesh.

'Chad,' she began, but his lips were moving against her neck, his breath rippling over her in little waves, and she felt herself stirred by unaccustomed desire.

She caught her breath before his lips closed possessively over hers. She could feel his heart pounding, and her own pulse raced in her ears. Instinctively she lifted her arms up and slid them around him, fully conscious of his rugged maleness. The dancing firelight and her own breathlessness combined to spin her dizzily into a whirlpool of sensation; her body seemed composed of a thousand electric nerve endings, each quivering with longing. Nothing in her life had prepared her for this yearning feeling, and she felt totally inflamed by the demands of Chad's lean hard body, hot against her own.

Suddenly conscious of where they were, she gasped and tried to pull away, but her writhing movement only incited Chad to a new level of passion. He renewed his possession of her lips and his level of arousal sparked her own response. She felt herself thrilling to their torture as his lips became more demanding, more searching.

She felt herself yielding to the most primitive force in the world, and to her utter surprise and dismay, she found herself enjoying it. Her wanton exhilaration signalled itself to Chad, because all at once his kisses changed in character, deepening into expressions of feelings far more passionate.

They had been half sitting, half leaning against the log behind them, but now they sank to the sand in a fluid motion, moving as one. His body lowered over hers until she could feel the full length of him easing on to her with a gentle pressure, so welcome. He rested on his elbows, his hands on either side of her face, cupping her cheeks gently. He released her lips for only a moment to murmur against them, looking down at her face honey-gold in the firelight, 'So beautiful,' before again capturing her willing lips with his.

She was conscious only of the weight of his body lying against hers, of the exquisite intimacy of warm flesh smooth against flesh. And then, as Chad's seeking fingers began to caress, to stroke, to explore the fabric of her brief swimsuit, she struggled back to consciousness, realising belatedly that things had gone too far. This shouldn't be happening, she thought wildly, as his kisses burned against her throat and downward to the firm skin between her breasts.

She fought her own surging emotion to come back to reality; she pushed the frenzied longing for the fulfilment of her passion to the outer reaches of her consciousness. She struggled against him, pushing him away, and in surprise, he eased his weight off her. She pulled herself to a sitting position, knowing with a sinking heart that this was madness; she couldn't allow such intimacies with a man she didn't love.

Chad leaned back against the log and stared at her, his lips full with passion. 'Why?' he asked quietly, when he saw that she had regained her composure.

'It wouldn't work,' she said, her voice low but determined.

'On the contrary, it seemed to be working very well,' he said with a trace of his old sauciness.

'That's not what I mean,' she said. 'You're talking about the physical part. I'm referring to the emotional part. There has to be more to it than just sex.'

Chad sat up and shrugged. He picked up a small twig and threw it into the dying fire where it flared briefly and then went out. 'Suppose you're right,' he said. 'What would it be like, this—this emotional feeling that you're talking about?'

Paige thought for a while, wondering why she felt compelled to share her innermost feelings. Somehow she wanted Chad to know how she felt about man–woman relationships—and in her present state of mind it didn't matter why. So at last she said, 'I suppose you could call it a communion of the spirit,' expecting him to laugh, but, surprising her, he didn't. 'It's a feeling between two people when they're completely as one,' she explained haltingly. 'Mentally as well as physically.'

It was what was missing with Stephen, what she had wanted to talk over with her aunts. Suddenly she was glad she hadn't shared her intimate feelings with either of the aunts after all; somehow it seemed appropriate to be talking of them with Chad. She had certainly never felt like broaching the subject with Stephen, even when he had asked her to share an apartment with him.

'And I suppose you've felt this "communion of the spirit?"' Chad was looking at her out of the corners of his eyes.

'No, not yet. But I will some day, with the right person.' It was what she had always believed, and she spoke with conviction. Beside her, Chad had an openly sceptical look on his face, replacing the unbridled passion of a few moments before.

They watched the fire for a moment, then Chad stood up and said abruptly, 'It sounds very nice, Paige. And I hope you find that person. In the meantime, though, maybe you could just settle for a common, ordinary, lustful communion of the body.' He was laughing at her after all.

Paige felt a monumental sense of disappointment. She should have known not to expect understanding, or even acceptance. She felt like an utter fool after so openly revealing what Chad obviously regarded as naïveté. To break the tension and to mask her own embarrassment, she threw a clump of dried-out seaweed at him, but she missed.

The swim she had intended to take seemed long overdue and more necessary than ever to completely quench the fire that Chad had ignited with his kisses. With one quick movement she stood and slipped out of the wrap-around skirt, fully conscious of Chad's eyes upon her scantily clad figure before she escaped as quickly as she could into the dark sanctuary of the night-time sea.

The water was much colder than she had imagined it would be, and she gasped as she felt its chill on her legs. But she needed its oblivion, and she dived directly beneath the surface of the moon's path, curving upward again before beginning to swim parallel to the shore with strong even strokes.

When she finally began to tire, she lay back and let the water buoy her up. The temperature no longer seemed too cold; in fact, it felt the exact temperature of her body. She closed her eyes and floated lazily, languidly, and let the soothing sea currents slide over her like waving banners of silk. In the distance, when she opened her eyes, she could see the eye of the bonfire like a beacon on the shore. Above her winked thousands of stars flung out across the sky. There was no sign of Chad; perhaps he had begun carrying the picnic food back to the Manse.

Paige's mind drifted with a ripple of excitement back to the scene on the beach with him. No doubt about it, he knew how to make love. This was no inexperienced boy; Chad knew all the little tricks of pleasing a woman. She shivered as she recalled the tenderness of his lips nipping at her throat, and she wondered how she would be able to resist his advances now that she knew how delightful his lovemaking could be. And she had reciprocated—she, who had never felt such abandon for any man. But then she had never met a man like Chad Smith, so roguish yet compelling, so masculine and so mysterious. Distrusting him as she did, how could she explain her ardent reactions to him, her almost-willingness to abandon her principles up there on the beach? She would have to re-intensify her determination to remain aloof, and she would have to make sure that opportunities for sexually charged contact were reduced.

A splash near by, a skimming movement, a head beside hers. Startled, frightened, she almost cried out, but to her immense relief she saw that it was only Chad.

'You frightened me,' she managed to say, treading water, reaching in vain for the sandy bottom with her foot. It was no use; the water was over her head.

'I didn't mean to startle you,' he said, beside her. He was so tall that he could stand up, even this far out.

The waves rose and fell gently, caressing their bodies, swirling around them in little eddies, glowing in the moonlight with a flickering phosphorescence. Droplets of water shimmered on Chad's face in the moonlight, lending a strangely iridescent quality to his dark skin. Paige dipped her head backward in the water and lifted it up again so that her long hair trailed sleekly down her back. Salt water trickled slowly down her shoulders, disappeared in the shadowed crevice between her breasts.

'You didn't say anything about a swim,' she said breathlessly, beginning to tire from the effort of staying afloat. 'I didn't think you'd worn a swimsuit.'

'Who needs one?' said Chad, smiling at her and lifting a damp eyebrow.

'You mean you're——'

'Naked as the day I was born,' he said wickedly. 'Want to see?'

'No,' she spluttered, swimming a few strokes away. She didn't know whether to be amused or outraged.

'You should try it some time,' he said, floating towards her. 'Such a sense of freedom. It would do you good to loosen up a bit.'

Paige eased into a slow sidestroke, keeping her eye on him. 'If I ever decide to loosen up, you'll be the first to find out,' she said dryly. She had to fight an urge to smile at his audacity.

'You might be interested to know that I sleep in the nude, too,' he volunteered, grinning as he swam a few strokes behind her.

Paige kicked a little fountain of water at him. 'I'm not the least bit interested in how you sleep. You can wear a space suit for all I care.' She turned languidly on her stomach and resumed a steady crawl, keeping her face in the water except when she came up for a breath. When she stopped to rest, she saw that he had kept up with her.

She'd had enough, she decided. It was time to go back to the Manse. She would swim back to the bonfire, dry herself, and get away from Chad and his absurd idea of humour as quickly as possible. She only hoped he would have the good sense to stay in the water until she was out of sight.

She began to swim again, but not for long. Suddenly, without the slightest warning, a crippling pain seized her right leg. Cramp! She stopped swimming, floundered, cried out. She had never felt such excruciating pain.

Chad, sensing trouble, stopped swimming immediately. Gone was his mischievous expression; it was replaced by a look of total concern.

'What's wrong?' he said, alarmed at the pinched whiteness of her face in the moonlight.

'My—my leg,' gasped Paige. 'A Cramp.'

'Can you reach bottom?'

With great effort she tried, with her unaffected leg, to stand. 'No,' she gasped.

'Let me hold you,' he commanded, sliding towards her through the black water.

'But you're——' She didn't like to think about his nude body suspended below the surface next to hers.

'You don't worry about things like that at a time like this!' he said sharply. He slid one hand smoothly around her waist and she could feel the warm skin of his chest against her arm. Beneath the water his leg brushed hers, sliding against it so softly that she might have mistaken it for a sea current if she hadn't known better. The thought of his nude body in contact with hers brought on a sensation so fiercely voluptuous that she almost forgot the terrible pain in her leg.

She wanted to push him away when she recognised that her feelings for him were again getting out of hand. But that would be foolish; she might not make it to shore without him. And now he was ordering her to wrap her arms around his neck, and she was doing it, wondering helplessly if she was obeying strictly out of a wish for survival or out of another equally compelling urge.

Chad was gliding his free hand down her body, pleasuring her unwittingly. When his probing fingers found the muscle in her calf knotted with tension, he asked, 'Is this it?'

Paige couldn't speak; she only nodded, her breath coming in short gasps. Carefully, with gentle fingers, he massaged the muscle. 'Try to relax,' was all he said, and she closed her eyes and laid her head against his broad shoulder, so warm and so reassuring.

Slowly the pain in her leg subsided. The muscle relaxed under Chad's soothing fingers.

'It's better,' she said at last.

'Think you can make it to shore?'

'Maybe,' she said, doubting it.

'I'll help you,' he said, and still holding her in his arms, her head resting against his shoulder, he carried her through the dark water towards the bonfire, now only a pile of glowing embers.

How could she not notice the droplets of seawater caught in the thick hair on his chest, glittering like jewels in the moonlight? How, with her head resting where it was, could she neglect to feel the strength in his arms as he clasped her to him? She gave in to it for a brief moment, letting herself submit to the involuntary tremor of passion that swept through her, letting go just enough to experience the nuances of movement in his body that told her that he was feeling it too. She was more conscious than ever of her own body betraying her emotions, of her own rich curves accommodating intimately to Chad's, of her long hair swirling damply against his muscular arm and clinging to his hard biceps, of cool seawater swirling against her hot swelling breasts.

Without thinking, she put out her tongue and touched it to the water-slick skin of his shoulder, tasting the sharp tang of salt. He stopped walking, swivelled his head and stared down at her questioningly. She, as surprised as he was at what she had done, only stared back at him, her lips parted, her breath coming in shallow gasps.

'Don't make it any more difficult for me than it already is!' he burst out, his voice harsh.

'I didn't think—I mean, I didn't know——' she babbled, all at once frightened at the fierceness in his face.

He was breathing hard, but he still held her close to him, their skins electric beneath the concealing water, his stomach muscles contracting convulsively. In a moment, the longest moment of her life, he had calmed himself and said more quietly, 'You should be able to swim to shore now. I'll wait here until you've gone.'

Paige nodded, still shaken. Wordlessly she slipped from his arms into the waiting water, skin sliding against skin. She ventured a few experimental strokes. 'I'm all right,' she said tremulously.

'Good. Swim slowly.' He stood and watched her, his

arms crossed across his muscular chest, his face impassive.

It wasn't far that she had to swim, but with his eyes upon her it seemed as though it were. When she reached the spot in front of the bonfire, she limped carefully out of the ocean and up the sandy beach to the log where she had left her skirt.

She picked it up and dried herself off with it the best she could. It had shaken her to see Chad finally lose his cool. She had thought he was completely unaffected by her own sexuality; she had thought she was the only one who suffered palpitations whenever they came near each other. Chad had always seemed so completely in control, and the knowledge that he wasn't able to keep his emotional distance any more than she was changed something fundamental in their relationship.

Somewhere beyond the edge of the black water Chad Smith was watching and waiting. Knowing that his eyes were upon her, she lifted her chin and walked haltingly up the beach, feeling a new emotion that she couldn't define.

CHAPTER FOUR

By the end of the next week Paige wondered if she had
been wrong about Chad's being a handyman. He threw
himself into refurbishing the Manse with an intensity
that surprised her. He was up every morning at dawn,
painting or hammering or noisily tearing away rotten
woodwork before they had even had a chance to eat
breakfast; his hyperactivity drove the aunts to distraction.

'But I thought you *wanted* this work done,' said
Paige, wrinkling her brow at Aunt Sophie and Aunt Biz
one evening over sherry.

'We did, dear, but Chad suddenly seems to have
taken it all so much to heart. He's been extremely
moody since he's been working on these projects, not at
all his old sunny-natured self,' said Aunt Biz.

'And the paint smell is everywhere,' Aunt Sophie
complained. 'I can't get away from it, and it simply
aggravates my allergies.' As if to prove her point, she
sniffed and managed to look completely miserable.

Paige was nonplussed by the aunts' attitude, and she
wondered if she had been wrong about putting Chad to
work. But actually she had only made the list, she
hadn't ever had a chance to goad Chad into following
it. He had taken over her list right after the night they
had cooked out on the beach; he had plunged into this
spell of frenzied activity the very next morning.

After that night when he had stood in the water and
watched her walk slowly up the hill to the Manse, Chad
had treated her with a coolness that was barely civil. No
more teasing banter, no long appraising looks that told
her he found her attractive. There had been no attempts
at lovemaking, a development that should have pleased

her; oddly, she felt disappointed rather than relieved.
He seemed to have clamped such a tight hold on his
emotions that he had shut her out of his life completely.

Considering the situation on St Albans, Paige should
have been grateful for this. But she found herself
wishing that their relationship could resume on a
friendly basis at least; after all, the aunts were too busy
with their own interests to be good company for her all
the time.

With Aunt Sophie and Aunt Biz, Chad at least tried
to maintain the same kind of lighthearted exchange they
had enjoyed before Paige's arrival, but Paige could see
that he often failed abysmally. Neither of the aunts
could understand the change in him, and even he
seemed totally annoyed with himself at times.
Nevertheless, Paige was interested to see that Chad
appeared to be genuinely fond of the aunts in spite of
his apparent inability to respond to their friendly
overtures.

At least, with the withdrawal of Chad's attentions,
she was able to think more lucidly about what to do
about Stephen McCall. Since she had come to St
Albans, she had found concentrating on the problem of
Stephen difficult. And even though she had thought she
had distanced herself from him, Stephen found a way of
effectively intruding on her life at St Albans.

Chad had evidently fallen into the habit of making
something of an event out of distributing the mail,
which he picked up in Brunswick whenever he had to
go there on an errand. On the first afternoon that they
heard him striding up the oyster-shell path and
shouting, 'Mail call!' Paige set aside her needlepoint and
joined an eager Aunt Sophie and Aunt Biz on the front
porch to greet him.

He stood below them, his fair hair slightly ruffled
over his forehead after the boat trip to the mainland.
Despite his recent coolness, he seemed determined to
make their receiving of the mail a good time for all.

'For you, Aunt Sophie,' he said, sounding doggedly cheerful, 'a new catalogue of kitchen gadgets. Maybe you'll find something in there that will un-boil pots,' and the catalogue was presented with a great flourish. 'For Aunt Biz—looks like another flyer from the garden supply store. Don't they know that you have plenty of fertiliser? The last load nearly scuttled the poor *Marsh Mallow* and broke the motor down besides.'

He shuffled through the envelopes. 'For Paige,' and he held out a letter from Stephen, the bold handwriting on the envelope unmistakably masculine. Chad stared at the handwriting for a moment, compressing his lips before thrusting it towards her. 'And for Paige,' as he handed her another identical one. 'For Paige, for Paige, for Paige, for Paige, and for Paige.' He knitted his eyebrows as he tossed her the envelopes. Forgotten was his effort to make mail call an event. He proceeded to distribute the rest of the mail hurriedly and with no attempt at further humour.

Paige noted that he did not call out his own mail, which consisted of several newspapers and a number of envelopes with windows in them, the kind of envelopes that usually contained bills. After an almost sullen goodbye, he went striding abruptly away down the path, his own portion of the mail tucked under his arm. Paige, whose eye had been caught by the stack of bills, couldn't help but wonder briefly what possible sort of expenses someone like Chad could have, living as simply as he did on this isolated island.

'Such a lot of letters,' Aunt Sophie said to her in open curiosity as she and Aunt Biz followed Paige into the cool recesses of the Manse. 'Your young man hasn't forgotten you, I see.'

'Mmm,' said Paige abstractedly, at this time not at all prepared to discuss Stephen or their relationship. The number of his letters had surprised her; she had thought that perhaps Stephen would not think of her if she were not available, and she couldn't imagine how he had gotten her address.

She had immersed herself so completely in her aunts' problems of keeping up the Manse, had become so caught up in the beauty around her, that it was hard to realise that she had a real life of her own in New York, a job to which she would eventually have to return, and Stephen, who, from the tone of his letters, was not simply going to fade away.

'Dearest Paige,' each of his letters began with identical fervour. And then he went on to write such things as, 'When you come back to New York, remind me to take you to a club called Elbert's Back Yard. I haven't been there (I wouldn't want to go without you, darling), but I've heard they have a talented comedian.' Darling? He had never called her darling; she wouldn't have allowed it. Or, more boldly, 'Let's take advantage of our airline passes and spend a long weekend in Bermuda,' a prospect which Paige found every bit as unlikely as the idea of moving in with him.

The letters only annoyed her. Stephen presumed too much; he had, in his typical high-handed manner, slotted her into his future. Now, after only a short time on St Albans, she could barely recall what Stephen looked like. She tried to picture him in her mind, and kept seeing an airline pilot's blue uniform surmounted by a featureless face and a shock of black curly hair. For a moment, she couldn't even remember what colour his eyes were, and when she tried to place them in his face, they turned out to be not blue, but flecked amber, like Chad's. Oh, it was impossible! It was patently clear to her that she didn't love Stephen, would never love Stephen. She'd write to him tomorrow and tell him that she wouldn't share his apartment.

Feeling much relieved by her decision, glad to have the matter over with, she returned to her needlepoint. As she drew the brightly-coloured yarn through the canvas, an activity that she usually found soothing, she found herself feeling vaguely concerned about something that she couldn't quite put her finger on. It had to do with the aunts, but she couldn't single out the exact reason why she felt so uneasy.

It wasn't until later that night that it struck her. At mail call, neither Aunt Biz nor Aunt Sophie had received any bills. Strange, considering that the mail included everything that had arrived for them at the post office all week. Even Chad had received bills, and she knew that in her absence, her own bills were piling up at her apartment in New York.

But then perhaps as they had grown older the aunts' requirements had dwindled. They had no need for an extensive wardrobe as Paige did, and living on St Albans where they grew most of their own food, their day-to-day expenses must be minimal. She put the aunts' business affairs out of her mind. It was none of her business, after all, and she had other important things to think about—how to word her reply to Stephen, for instance.

She composed a brief letter the next morning. 'I'm sorry, Stephen,' she wrote, 'but I've been thinking over your suggestion that we live together, and I feel that it would be something that we'd both eventually regret. In fact, I think that we should stop seeing each other altogether.' She paused before signing her name; 'Love, Paige' seemed inappropriate, so she simply scrawled her name at the bottom of the paper and sealed it quickly in an envelope. It seemed tremendously important to her that Stephen find out the truth about their relationship immediately, which meant that she would have to get her letter in the mail at the next possible chance.

Chad had announced his intention to do some surf-casting that morning, hoping to catch fresh fish for their dinner, so she walked down to the beach with her letter.

He eyed her cautiously as she approached, scarcely

seeming delighted to see her. If ever she had seen an about-face change in anyone, it was in Chad. Well, it was necessary for her to talk with him; besides, it was ridiculous for them both to be inhabiting this small island without exchanging a few words now and then. At least they should be able to speak of practical matters, if not personal ones.

Chad was barefoot, wearing only dark green swim trunks and an unbuttoned yellow short-sleeved shirt. He stood beside the long fishing pole where he had stuck it into the sand, watching the slack line disappearing far out in the sea, beyond the trough where the waves broke before running up on shore.

'Have you had any luck?' she asked when she stood beside him. There was a stiff breeze today; it caught and flung her words backward. The pungent odour of salt and seaweed blew about them.

Chad shook his head ruefully. 'None at all. Not even a bite.' His eyes rested on her, remote and shuttered, effectively making a stranger of her.

Despite his remoteness, she smiled at him. Perhaps if she made an effort they could still be friends.

'I'd help if I could, but I don't know anything about surf fishing. I really just came to ask you when you thought you'd be taking the *Marsh Mallow* to Brunswick again.'

Chad raised his eyebrows. 'Why? Do you need to go to the mainland?'

'Not really, but I do have a letter I'd like you to mail next time you go.'

'A letter? I'll be happy to mail it for you. Aunt Biz will want me to go to the paint store again soon, perhaps tomorrow morning. I'll mail it for you then.' He nodded towards the envelope in her hands. 'If that's the letter, I'll take it now. I have several things of my own that need to go off tomorrow.'

Paige handed him the envelope, and he skimmed the address hurriedly. His face tightened perceptibly for a moment, but then he bent over and tucked the letter into his tackle box. When he straightened, his face was devoid of expression.

She decided to make a stab at conversation, hoping to draw him out of his shell. 'I like the way the portico looks, now that you've scraped and painted it,' she ventured.

'Mmm. Thanks.' Chad stared out over the ocean, his eyes locked on the seam where sea met sky.

'Aunt Biz seems to have decided on a colour for the upstairs hallway. Oyster white, I believe.'

'Good.' His eyes remained on the horizon.

He was snubbing her, plain and simple. Clearly, as far as he was concerned, there was to be no return to the joking camaraderie of her first days on the island. Paige felt embarrassment rising inside her. What a ninny she was! She had effectively discourage his advances, and now he probably thought she was making a play for him! No wonder he didn't want anything to do with her!

She turned to go, brushing aside a wisp of hair that the wind had blown across her face.

'Paige,' he said suddenly, and something in the tone of his voice made her whirl and stare at him across the space between them.

'Tell Aunt Sophie that if I haven't delivered any fish by five o'clock to go ahead and cook the casserole that she'd planned.' Whatever emotion she had thought she'd heard in his voice, it wasn't there now. Though neither of them had moved, the space between them grew wider and seemed occupied by something heavier than air.

'I'll tell her,' she said. Then, feeling inexplicably disappointed, she turned and began the long walk back to the Manse.

Later, she was in the kitchen assembling the ingredients for scalloped tomatoes when she heard Chad stamping sand off his feet on the back porch before he came in. He seemed taken aback to find her in the kitchen instead of Aunt Sophie. He set a newspaper-wrapped bundle on the countertop.

'So you caught some fish after all!' she said, and to her own ears it seemed that she spoke too loudly and with forced gaiety. 'Aunt Sophie and Aunt Biz and I all agreed that we were in the mood for seafood. Why, we haven't had any since the crabs we ate the night of the party, which is ridiculous when you consider where we live!' she knew she was prattling, and she stopped short, busying herself selfconsciously with unwrapping the layers of newspaper from the fish.

Chad regarded her from under his eyebrows, something troubled in his gaze. He was standing within arm's length; Paige could have reached out and touched him, and crazily she felt the urge to do so. She fumbled with the newspaper, wholly unnerved by the way he simply stood and stared at her. For a moment she felt sure that he was about to take her in his arms, and her pulse throbbed in anticipation.

But, 'I'll be back at dinnertime,' he said shortly, then he turned quickly on his heel and strode out of the door without even a vestige of politeness.

Stung, Paige stared at the place where he had stood, her anticipation falling away, tears unbelievably stinging her eyes. His churlishness had hurt her feelings terribly, and for the first time she began to think that she cared about his attitude more than she had ever admitted to herself.

Day after day, watching him working with a vengeance at the tedious chores around the Manse, she had longed for the return of his lighthearted jokes, his teasing, the joy that he had brought to the lives of her aunts. She hated the thought that she was responsible for the change in Chad, and not only for the sake of her aunts. She felt a stab of self-pity; she and Chad could have found some level on which they could have related, if only . . .

After blinking away the sudden tears, there was nothing to do but to continue to unwrap the fish, which was insulated in layers of newspaper and then wrapped in waxed paper. In her unhappy state of mind, Paige wouldn't have noticed the name of the newspaper if a broad headline about an airline hadn't caught her eye. Why, it was the *Wall Street Journal*! This newspaper, all business, certainly wasn't what she expected to see on St Albans, where business and everyday life seemed so far removed.

Her eyes picked out the date at the top of the page. It was a recent date, only about a week ago. Then she recalled the armload of newspapers that Chad had carried back to the Sea House with him the day he had fetched the mail from Brunswick. Identically folded and wrapped, they all must have been the *Wall Street Journal*. How odd. Chad seemed to be the last person in the world to be interested in such a staid and businesslike paper, the bulwark of the financial world. Like a lot of other little things about his character and personality, it simply did not fit in with the image that he conveyed on St Albans.

As she cut up the tomatoes, Paige forced herself to ban thoughts of his physical presence from her mind. Instead she puzzled over the inequities in his character and personality. They didn't make sense, nothing added up. Now that she had dispatched the problem of Stephen McCall, she found herself growing concerned all over again about Chad Smith. Certainly he still bore watching; she found that she couldn't, despite his recent conversion to the perfect handyman, completely rid herself of her initial distrust of him.

The next morning Aunt Biz announced her intention to go to Brunswick to buy the new paint and asked Chad if he would accompany her. Chad, who was painting the downstairs hall that day, set aside his paint brush. 'I'll go, so you won't have to,' he said. 'Since you know the paint shade, I can buy the paint and bring it home. Besides,' and he eyed Paige meaningfully, 'I need to mail some letters at the post office.' But Aunt Biz insisted that she needed to talk to the paint store manager about mixing a special shade for the downstairs powder room, and so the two of them set off together for Brunswick in the *Marsh Mallow*.

After Paige and Aunt Sophie had watched the two of them disappear towards the wide green marshes of Little St Simons, they made their way slowly back up the oyster-shell path towards the Manse.

'I declare, Paige,' said Aunt Sophie between sneezes, 'you'll have to amuse yourself this morning. My allergy has been acting up worse than ever, and I'm planning to stay in my room all day, as far away from the paint fumes as possible.'

'Don't worry about me, Aunt Sophie,' said Paige. 'I'm capable of finding something to do. You go ahead and rest.' Aunt Sophie tottered off to her room, sneezing all the way.

For a while, Paige worked on the old treadle sewing machine, which she had dragged out of the closet and set up in her room. She had found brightly coloured fabrics in the closet, and had completed several pillows for the couch in the study. She was a fast seamstress; before long, she had completed one more pillow and decided to close up the sewing machine. It was much too pretty a day to remain inside.

She stood for a moment on the balcony outside her room, breathing deeply of the tangy sea air. The ocean was a glistening shade of aquamarine, sparkling in the bright golden sunlight. Overhead a flock of seagulls wheeled and dipped and called querulously to one another with high-pitched voices.

An idea gripped her, and she went to her closet and rummaged around on the top shelf until her fingers found what they sought. It was her own sketchbook, the one she had placed there five years ago when she had last visited St Albans. Quickly she leafed through it, stopping every now and then to study a drawing. They were good, she thought with surprise, wondering why she had never further developed her talent. She would like to try her hand at sketching again, and this morning was as good a time as any.

Her drawings five years ago had been varied—here she had sketched some of the plants native to the island, a thistle, bachelor's button, holly. And there was a drawing, never finished, of the tiny houses in the fishermen's village on the north end of the island. And here was a funny one, almost a cartoon, of a pelican with a droll look about him because his bill was too full of fish. She might someday work some of these sketches into needlepoint designs; she had already designed several original needlepoint canvases for her friends, and had in fact developed her talent into a rather lucrative sideline to supplement her airline pay-cheque. She suspected that there would be a market for such original designs as these.

She tucked the sketchbook under her arm and headed downstairs. Today, with Chad gone, would be the perfect time to walk to the promontory and sit in front of the Sea House to sketch.

She stopped in the kitchen, wrinkling her nose at the pervasive smell of paint, and found a chunk of Brie and some crackers to carry with her. There wasn't much to drink, but she filled an insulated jug with fruit juice and set off towards the beach.

She had worn her briefest bikini, the jade green one with the high-cut legs and the tiny top. Her hair was brushed back behind her ears and bounced loosely around her shoulders as she walked. The sand felt hot on the soles of her feet; she wished she'd worn sandals. But, she reflected, she really didn't need them when she could walk at the edge of the surf.

Ahead of her, little sandpipers scampered away on skinny legs; a curious sand crab poked his head out of his hole and just as quickly retreated. Finally Paige rounded the curve and came upon the Sea House. It stood on the point like a squat grey sentinel, nestled amid the salt grass and sea oats on the dunes. As she approached she could see that Chad had cleared away the tangle of undergrowth and weeds that had once threatened to envelop the building.

Curiously she walked up to the Sea House and peered in one of the windows. A thin film of salt spray obscured her vision; she rubbed at it with the towel she carried.

Chad had done a good job with the interior, as much as she could see of it, anyway. She recognised the massive fireplace that took up one whole wall, built like the rest of the house of round grey ballast stones. Above it, its woolly texture an effective contrast against the smoothness of the stones, hung a hooked rag rug in spiralling shades of red, orange and yellow.

He hadn't done any painting here as far as she could see, and the floor was still wide wooden planks, highly polished now. She saw a bed, piled high with colourful pillows on top of a striped wool serape, against another wall. Soft fibre rugs accented the floor, there were two comfortable-looking armchairs, and she noted several ship models on the top of a pair of well-stocked bookshelves. She recognised a long wide table, piled high with papers, as having once been in the study at the Manse. Altogether the Sea House looked like a comfortable bachelor pad.

And of course the view was breathtaking. Page walked around the front of the Sea House and tried the door, which was locked. She might have known; Chad wouldn't want any intruders. She turned and stood on the front porch, watching the sea. This was the perfect place to sit and sketch. She sat down, leaned against the low wall encircling the porch, and took out her pad and pencils. Before long she was totally absorbed in transferring a ready-made still-life—an unusually twisted piece of driftwood, a prettily shaped shell, and an obliging butterfly—to paper.

When she had completed her drawing to her satisfaction, she stood and stretched and decided on a quick swim. She ran into the water, but this time she remembered not to swim any distance from shore. She didn't want to take the chance of being crippled by a cramp again, especially when she was alone.

By the time she came out of the water she felt thoroughly relaxed. Deciding not to towel herself dry but let herself drip dry in the sun, she sat on her towel and ate the Brie and the crackers and drank the fruit juice. The sun beat down, its warmth suffusing her muscles and making them feel stretched and loose. Paige hadn't realised how totally absorbed she had become in her drawing; she must have been completely wound up. It felt good to let the sun bake the tightness out of her muscles and lull her into a state of well-being.

She finished eating, capped the jug containing the juice, and lay down on her back. The sun was a hot red circle behind her eyelids; she let her facial muscles go slack.

She wanted to be tanned when she went back to the city, and here she had the opportunity to get an early start on a suntan that would be the envy of all her friends. She sighed and twisted to get more comfortable—if only the top of her bikini didn't bind her breasts so tightly! Well, she could solve that; she could take it off. Then she smiled to herself. She would never go topless. In fact, she was known to be so modest that her girl friends often joked that Paige Brownell hid in a closet to change her mind!

On the other hand, though, who was here to see her? Chad and Aunt Biz were safely in Brunswick, and there was a good chance that their arrival back on St Albans would be delayed by motor trouble—it usually was. Aunt Sophie, of course, was staying in her room.

Why not? Paige didn't stop to think about it any more. She sat up, blinking as she opened her eyes, and reached behind her to untie the brief bikini bra. Her bare breasts, startlingly white against her suntan, felt free and unencumbered. Feeling delightfully risqué. Paige tossed the bra to one side, lay back again and closed her eyes. The sun on her nipples felt welcome and warm. Like the touch of the lover she had never had, thought Paige whimsically.

The steady swish of the sea upon the shore, the lazy cries of the shore birds, the sultry heat of the afternoon sun on her bare skin—all combined to make her feel drowsy. She felt sedated, unable to resist the inexorable temptation to slide into sleep. She stirred once, settling more comfortably into the sand, then slipped into a dream about a high-masted sailing boat, sails unfurled in the wind, and a tall golden-haired man who just happened to look very much like . . .

'Chad!' With a cold shock vibrating through her, she stared up at him from her position on the sand. His eyes, seething with an intensity that at first she couldn't fathom, blazed down her body and took in her small breasts, rounded with taut upthrust nipples, then moved down to her flat stomach, stopping at the green triangle of material that saved her from being completely nude.

Paige sat up abruptly, reaching about in her embarrassment for the top of her swimsuit. Where was it? Surely it couldn't have gone too far, she had only put it to one side—and then with a sinking feeling she realised that he was kneeling on it.

He hadn't taken his eyes off her, and he continued to drink in her nakedness like a thirsty man who had been too long in the desert. Vainly she tried to cover herself with her arms, but it did no good. Somehow, though she had tried to avoid it, her eyes met his, caught and held, spun away into their bright shining amber depths. Looking at him was like gazing at the sun; his eyes were all-powerful, hypnotic, magnetic. She almost wanted to close her eyelids against their brilliance, but she couldn't. She could only let herself be caught up in their spell.

'Isn't it enough that you're here to tempt me every day of my life?' he said hoarsely. 'Must you put yourself on display in front of the house where I live?'

'But I didn't——'

'You did, and I'm not sorry,' he said, and before she could reply, his body had closed the gap between them and his arms were around her, crushing her to him in a mind-shattering intimacy, exquisite in its raw sensuality.

His kiss was hot and ravenous, so demanding that she felt as though she were being swept into a firestorm of urgent longing. Paige found herself responding with complete lack of inhibition. Her breasts swelled and ached, her nipples peaked and hardened against the silkiness of the soft hair on his chest. His impassioned hands caressed her back, gently at first, then stroking harder and harder until all at once he stopped, brought them forward, and gently cupped one tempting breast in each hand, his thumbs teasing their rosy tips into sensuous peaks.

'I've dreamed of you like this,' he said unsteadily, and he lowered his lips to one roseate nipple.

Paige was a maelstrom of feeling as she looked down at his hair, shining in the sun, and saw his mouth moving on her breast. The sight of his lips pressed to this intimate place moved her beyond words and she moaned softly. He looked up at her, a question in his eyes.

'I didn't hurt you, did I?'

'No,' she whispered.

'Do you want me to stop?' he demanded, and it was unthinkable to say yes. It was also unthinkable to say no, however, so she hung in indecision, wanting to go on savouring the closeness of Chad's body.

When she said nothing, he took advantage of the chance to press his lips to hers once more, and again she matched his ardour, wondering if her defences were totally destroyed. Chad teased her with tiny kisses on her face, everywhere but on her lips, which craved them; he tortured her with little licking kisses on her throat, which thrilled to them; he wandered his kisses downward to the cleft between her breasts, holding them in his hands so that their roundness caressed his face.

He kissed the undersides of her breasts, her bare midriff; then, without pausing, he eased her back on the towel and slid his hand lightly over her stomach to rest at the top of her bikini bottom; the elastic gave easily to admit his fingers and his hand closed over one smooth hip. Paige knew she should stop him, and now; but she wanted to allow herself just a few more seconds, a few more minutes of these sensations, so deliciously erotic.

And she didn't only want to receive pleasure, she also wanted to give it. Her fingers slid through his golden hair, caressed his neck, fluttered across the muscular contours of his back, teased the taut muscles above the top of his swim trunks.

His lips lifted from hers long enough to let her gasp, and he opened his eyes and peered down at her. 'Do you feel it yet?' he asked fiercely. 'The communion of spirit that you told me about?'

In the silence that followed his totally unexpected question, Paige heard the sharp cry of seagulls overhead, the curling rush of the waves to the shore. She stared at his face above her, the handsome mask that persisted in hiding the mystery that was Chad Smith. She felt a stab of pain somewhere in the region of her heart. Despite her craving for him, despite her longing to gratify this passion that seemed to penetrate to the deepest core of her being, despite everything, she could not lie.

'No,' she breathed, devastated.

He leaned back and stared at her. 'It's still important to you, though, isn't it? Isn't it?' His voice was husky and his hands were on her shoulders. He gave her a little shake.

'Yes, it's important,' she murmured despairingly, her senses jarred. She felt on the verge of tears.

'Ah, Paige,' he said with anguish, those two words seeming to express all the melancholy he had felt since his retreat into remoteness, and he rolled over on his back until he lay face up on the sand, one arm thrown up over his eyes.

She lay beside him, overwrought, painfully aware of her half-nakedness, her heart hammering in her chest.

When he spoke, his voice had returned to its normal tone, and he had regained complete control. He looked over at her, his head still resting on the sand. 'Wrap that towel around you,' he said unemotionally, almost indifferently. 'You'd better leave.'

Paige could no longer restrain her tears. He was sending her away. 'The top of my swimsuit is underneath you,' she said, turning her face away so that he couldn't see her eyes. She felt a monumental sense of disappointment and despair.

Chad found the top of her swimsuit for her and put it in her hand, then without another word he stood and strode into the Sea House, slamming the door behind him.

Numbly she pulled herself together, fumbling with the ties of her bikini top, trying to get a grip on herself. She gathered up her belongings and almost ran down the beach away from the Sea House and Chad Smith.

She paused in the grove of trees bordering the beach before climbing the incline to the Manse. It wouldn't do for the aunts to see her in such a state of agitation; she must calm herself before seeing either of them. She wasn't sure how either would respond to the knowledge that she and Chad were more involved than Paige had ever intended to be.

Finally, when she was able to still her rapidly beating heart, she let herself quietly into the Manse, hoping that she'd be able to sneak up to her room without having to manufacture polite conversation for the aunts' benefit.

She knew at once that this was not to be, however. The Manse was a flurry of activity with Aunt Biz barking out orders to Aunt Sophie and Aunt Sophie, flustered and holding a rumpled handkerchief to her red nose, scurrying about trying to obey.

Paige stood in the centre of the wide downstairs hall and took it all in for a few minutes, then asked hesitantly, 'What's going on?'

Aunt Biz stopped in the middle of the staircase with a pile of clean clothes in her arms and looked down at Paige in mild surprise. 'Why, Paige, I hope you don't mind. We've been invited to visit a friend in Macon, and we're going. We'll be leaving first thing in the morning.'

CHAPTER FIVE

IT wasn't just to visit their girlhood friend Emma, confided Aunt Sophie between sneezes, but to get away from the horrid paint odour. They usually went to Macon in October; however, the letter they had received from Emma that morning had invited them to come now because she had other plans for the fall.

'We hope you don't mind, Paige,' Aunt Biz said, 'but we'll be back after the paint inside the house has had a chance to dry. And we'll still have time to visit with you after we return.'

'Are you sure you wouldn't like to come along with us?' ventured Aunt Sophie. 'You remember Emma. She'd love to have you.'

Paige did remember Emma, a soft sweet vapid lady who lived in a large white-columned house in the country. Paige found Emma utterly boring. Give up the golden pleasures of St Albans to go to Macon? 'Thank you, but no,' she told the aunts as kindly as she could. Besides, she planned to sew new curtains for the downstairs powder room.

So that was why she stood again on the ramshackle dock, shepherding the aunts and all their luggage into the *Marsh Mallow*, and avoiding the eyes of an unusually morose Chad Smith, whose unspoken opinion seemed to be that he'd be much relieved if she were leaving the island along with her aunts.

She sneaked a look at him when she was sure he wasn't looking, noting the wide purple smudges beneath his eyes, the grim set of his mouth, his refusal to look at her. She breathed a sigh of relief when the boat, with Chad at the tiller, chugged away from St Albans and disappeared in the twisting channels through the marsh grass.

The episode yesterday on the beach should never have happened, she reflected with embarrassment. It was all her fault for throwing caution to the winds and acting immodestly. She had learned her lesson; she would not provoke Chad again. From now on she would remain decently covered. Obviously they shared a strong physical attraction for one another, but it didn't have to become an obsession. And judging from Chad's unfeeling dismissal of her yesterday, it was no obsession with him.

She spent a quiet day with her sketchbook, staying in the vicinity of the Manse. Later on during her visit she would go farther afield, perhaps take the Mule down to the fishermen's village to see how it had changed with time. There were tabby ruins of several old settlers' cabins hidden in the deep underbrush somewhere on the island. One day she would go exploring and find them.

During the afternoon—she wasn't sure what time— she heard the unmistakable putt-putt of the *Marsh Mallow*. So Chad had returned, she thought, and she was relieved. At least he wasn't stranded in a channel somewhere between St Albans and Brunswick, tinkering with the *Marsh Mallow*'s temperamental motor. She resumed her drawing. Chad would most likely spend the afternoon working at the Manse, and she'd stay away until he had gone.

When she had tired of drawing, she folded up her sketch pad and headed back to the Manse. She found her mail stacked neatly on the doormat, courtesy of Chad. More letters from Stephen. She tore them open impatiently, frowning as she saw herself again addressed as 'darling', resisting the impulse to tear the lot of them into shreds. Obviously Stephen had not yet received the letter she'd sent.

She was surprised when she went through the front door and found that Chad had not been working and was not finishing the painting of the downstairs hall as she had expected. A quick walk through the rest of the house told her that he hadn't been working on any other projects, either. Well, he'd looked very tired in the morning; perhaps he had decided to take the afternoon off. As in when the cat's away, the mice will play, she thought wryly.

She decided to heat up last night's leftovers for her solitary dinner. She removed the oyster stew from the refrigerator and dumped it into a small pan before turning on the burner of the big old-fashioned electric range. Her hand was still on the switch when she heard an ear-shattering pop as a fist-sized spark leaped out of the centre of the burner. The air was filled with the acrid stench of scorched electrical wire.

Without hesitation she ran to the pantry where the fuse box was located and pulled the master switch, plunging the house into darkness. She stood for a moment, her heart thumping, before she was able to see sufficiently to move back into the kitchen and throw the kitchen curtains open to admit the light of the moon.

Something was wrong with the range, no doubt about it. She fumbled around in the kitchen for a flashlight, but she couldn't find one. She wondered if it would be dangerous to pull the master switch on again, if the range would again emit sparks. After a few moments' thought, she decided not to risk it.

Much as she disliked the idea, she would have to find Chad. In the aunts' absence, they were both responsible for the Manse and St Albans, and perhaps he'd know what to do.

She headed down the oyster-shell path, her feet crunching with each step. There were two ways to reach the Sea House, and this time she decided to take the back way, the trail through the woods that approached the Sea House from behind. She went into the forest, a deep green glade, still and veiled in Spanish moss.

The sandy path was strewn with dry dead leaves and stippled with moonlight. Paige had once tried to figure out if the beach approach or the woods approach to the

Sea House took longer; she had finally concluded that they both consumed about the same amount of time. The choice simply depended on the mood one was in.

Tonight she was definitely in the mood for the forest. Here and there night creatures scurried about their business in the underbrush, but they didn't alarm her. Overhead an owl hooted from the branch of a spreading oak tree, his call ending on a wistful note before he flapped noisily away in the direction of the salt marsh.

Paige could see the lights of the Sea House long before she reached it, and they reassured her that Chad was there. She had often wondered how Chad spent his spare time; he never lingered at the Manse long after dinner, preferring to get away early. In fact, it had always seemed to her that Chad looked forward to his evenings, though she never understood why. Yet she knew that he had never left the island at night; she would have been sure to hear the agonised putter of the *Marsh Mallow*'s motor. Perhaps he simply liked to read good books, and at this thought she smiled. The idea of a rugged good-looking slightly raffish bachelor like Chad spending every evening in his slippers and bathrobe, his feet propped up as he read a good book, was more than a bit ridiculous.

The Sea House stood on the promontory, its grey stones washed silver in the moonlight. A freshening breeze gently ruffled the stalks of sea oats, and beyond the sand the surf tumbled over on itself in a froth of white bubbles.

Paige walked carefully along the side of the Sea House towards the front door, and she glanced in the first window almost without a thought. She stopped short, however, when she realised with a jolt that she was interrupting something.

Chad leaned over the long table, his fair hair falling over his forehead as it so often did, wearing nothing but a pair of cut-off denims. One hand was on the table, the other rested on the back of a straight chair, lightly touching the shoulder of a girl who sat gazing up at him, a smile playing across her features.

Paige didn't recognise the girl, but then she knew so few people here. Chad's guest was pretty in a feline sort of way, a redhead, with a straight, pointed nose and thin eyebrows winging upward across a wide brow. No freckles, Paige noted, which was unusual in a redhead. Unless, of course, she wasn't a natural redhead. The girl wore a strapless aqua terrycloth sunsuit cut low across the top, revealing an impressive cleavage. As Paige stood stunned, staring in the window, the girl slowly turned her head and, catlike, fixed her eyes on Paige

'Chad, look!' said the girl. 'Someone is watching us!'

Chad glanced up quickly, apprehension in his eyes. An intruder on St Albans was unusual and cause for alarm. When he saw who it was, relief slid across his face. 'Relax, Glynis,' he said. 'It's only Paige.'

Paige had the strongest urge to bolt and run. She had no choice, however, if she wanted to avoid making a complete fool of herself. With as much dignity as she could muster in the circumstances, she walked to the door of the Sea House. Chad arrived there first, unbolted the door, and stood on the threshold looking down at her with an expression of uneasiness.

She stared up at him, unsure of her welcome. She had had no idea he ever entertained women visitors—the island's remoteness seemed to preclude that—and the girl's presence here had caught her unawares. Chad with a woman was a possibility that had never crossed her mind, and she found herself feeling left out, indignant, and yes, a bit jealous. Her thoughts whirled around inside her brain like a miniature cyclone, leaving her tongue-tied and unable to speak.

It was finally Chad who spoke first. 'Well, what is it?' he said brusquely and with more than a hint of impatience.

'I—I didn't mean to interrupt,' she said lamely,

feeling like an errant schoolgirl. The girl in the chair had swivelled around and was chilling her with the stare from her turquoise-blue eyes. In spite of the night's warmth, Paige shivered.

'Don't be ridiculous,' he said, and to her immense surprise he took her arm and pulled her inside where she blinked in the unaccustomed light. 'I don't like to leave the door open,' he explained curtly. 'The sand gnats are out in swarms tonight. Paige, this is Glynis McGuire from St Simons. Glynis, Paige Brownell.'

Glynis murmured a greeting and rested her chin on her hand. She continued to stare at Paige as though she were a piece of flotsam washed up on the beach. Well, she probably looked it, thought Paige unhappily, reaching up to smooth her windblown hair, suddenly conscious of her wrinkled smock-top and too-short shorts.

She decided not to linger at the Sea House any longer than necessary. 'Chad,' she said abruptly, 'there's a problem with the electric range. I turned it on and there was a terrific popping noise as well as a spark, so I ran and pulled the master switch to cut off the electricity. The trouble is that I don't know whether it's safe to turn it back on.'

Chad ran a hand through his hair. 'You want me to come look at it?'

'Well, yes. You see, I'm without electricity at the Manse and——'

'And you think I know all about appliances and electrical systems, is that right? I've seen the wiring at the Manse at various times when I've been down in the basement. It's positively medieval.'

'But as the handyman——' protested Paige.

'As the handyman, I should be able to fix it. I know. And I also know that I don't understand a damned thing about electrical wiring.'

'You mean you won't even come to look at it?' Paige's voice rose on a note of panic; she couldn't live in the Manse without electricity.

Chad heaved a sigh of annoyance. Glynis grinned to herself and turned away from them, making a show of busying herself with a pile of papers on the table. Finally, when the silence grew unbearable, Chad said, 'I'll come and look at it. But later, after I've taken Glynis home.'

Glynis looked up sharply from her papers. 'You're not taking me home! I thought you said——'

Chad waved a hand to silence her. 'Never mind what I said. Gather up those papers and I'll run you back to St Simons in the boat. I'll talk to you about them some other time.'

With a disgruntled look, Glynis began shuffling papers into a folder, taking her time.

'Do you want to ride along in the boat with us?' Chad addressed this question to Paige.

'No, thanks,' she said, making an effort to keep her voice even.

'We'll walk you back to the Manse,' he said.

'That's not necessary,' she assured him. 'I know my way around St Albans, even at night.'

'I'm sure you do,' he said smoothly, 'but we're going that way anyway. We'll see you safely there.'

He found a flashlight in a basket beside the door and slipped a knit tee-shirt over his head. When Glynis indicated that she was ready, she and Paige preceded Chad out the door and he locked it securely behind them. He took the lead, swinging the flashlight as he walked, casting lopsided shadows in their path as they made their way through the woods towards the Manse. They proceeded in single file, Paige following Chad and Glynis behind Paige.

At the back door of the Manse, Chad turned to Paige. 'Do you know where the candles are?' She shook her head, wishing unreasonably, childishly, that he wouldn't go, leaving her alone in the dark. 'Here, take the flashlight,' he said, his tone businesslike. 'Look in the drawers in the sideboard in the dining room. Aunt

Sophie likes to eat by candlelight on occasion, and I think I've seen her storing the candles there. Matches too.' For a moment he looked as though he might spare her a grin, but instead he turned towards Glynis, who murmured a goodbye to Paige and walked ahead of him, hips swaying in her short sunsuit, towards the dock.

Paige stood on the porch, watching them disappear into the darkness, listening, when their footsteps had died, to the chirrup of crickets in the bushes. She almost ran after them, calling to them to take her along, but she thought better of it. She had already interrupted their evening; she had intruded where she was clearly not welcome.

Heaving a sigh, she turned and went back inside the Manse, fixing the offending electric range with a baleful look. Nothing to be done about it now, she thought grimly. She poured her oyster stew back in its plastic container and opened the refrigerator, also electric and also not working until she felt it safe to turn the master switch back on. She shoved the stew inside and quickly shut the door to preserve the low temperature. It was a good thing that she'd lost her appetite; she couldn't cook anything at the moment anyway.

The flashlight was a help, enabling her to locate the candles and the matches without any problem. She struck a match and it flared in the darkness, illuminating for a moment the spooky shapes of the big antique dining-room furniture. Paige wondered disconsolately what she could do with herself until Chad returned. St Albans wasn't the most comforting place in total darkness; the Manse was downright scary, with the big high-ceilinged rooms disappearing into blackness and with the large bulky furniture leaning in on her from every side.

Never before had she noticed how the wind blew through the trees outside, whipping little branches against the upstairs windows with a staccato clacking sound. One tree limb, perhaps on the big oak tree outside the dining room, creaked alarmingly. It was enough to give anybody the shivers. Paige stared forlornly at the candle she'd lit. It wasn't bright enough to dispel the ghosts that seemed hidden around every corner.

But she was being silly, foolish; nothing was going to happen to her, and besides, she'd never been afraid of the dark on St Albans, had she? Maybe she should go to her room and try to sleep, but she discarded the idea almost immediately. It was much too early to retire for the evening, and besides, if she did that, she'd just have to get up again when Chad arrived.

Finally she settled on a glass of sherry in the parlour, a ritual she had thought she would give up while the aunts weren't here. But the sherry was sure to have a calming effect on her, and tonight she certainly needed it.

The candle on the mantel in its tall old-fashioned sterling silver candlestick lit the parlour with a golden glow, dispelling some, but not all of the shadows. She splashed sherry from its cut-glass decanter into a stemmed monogrammed glass, then wandered over to sit on the high old Victorian couch to wait for Chad, looking apprehensively over her shoulder before she sat down. Did she hear a faint scrabbling noise overhead? But Aunt Biz wouldn't put up with such a nuisance as mice. Squirrels, then. That's what they were. Squirrels, jumping from the branches of the oak tree to the roof. Paige pulled her feet up on the couch and huddled there, wishing Chad would hurry.

The upholstery material on the couch was comforting against her skin, soft velvet. She thought that she should be sitting here, sweetly composed, in a long red silken gown, and not lumping nervously about in this rumpled smock and her oldest shorts. She smiled to herself at the thought. Perhaps long red silken gowns had been apropos in the aunts' heyday, but things had changed.

Seeking to occupy her mind with something, anything, to get it off the spookiness of the Manse in darkness, she puzzled over Glynis. Perhaps Glynis's presence explained Chad's usual eagerness to return to the Sea House every evening. No, that was impossible. Glynis could never have arrived and left St Albans without either Paige or the aunts being aware of her. Unless she was completely mistaken, this was Glynis's only visit to St Albans. But why had Chad invited her? There were all those papers, Chad's papers, that Glynis had made such a point of sorting. The papers only increased Paige's curiosity about Chad; there had been quite a stack of them, typed and double-spaced, piled high like a thick manuscript.

Paige finished the sherry and went to pour herself another glass. She felt much more serene now and slightly less nervous about being alone in the big house, almost prepared to tackle the problems of the Manse's monster electrical wiring system when Chad returned. She peered at her wristwatch, but it was too hard to read in this mellow half-light. It seemed as though Chad had been gone a very long time.

They were really such small glasses, she thought as she poured out still another glass of sherry, her third. Upstairs on the landing the grandfather clock chimed its mellifluous song, and somewhere in the middle Paige lost count and thought, oh well, what difference does it make what time it is?

She kicked off her leather sandals and lifted her feet up on the tiny footstool, its cover designed and worked in crewel by Aunt Sophie. Halfway through the glass of sherry she set it down on the little chest beside the couch and closed her eyes. Sherry was nice, she thought, wrapped up in the cosy cocoon of its warmth. Too bad that when the aunts were here they never got as far as a third glass.

If Chad had knocked when he came in, she would have had ample warning, but he didn't. Half dozing as she was, she hadn't even heard the chugging of the motor as the *Marsh Mallow* approached the St Albans dock. He must have stood watching the candlelight flicker across her face, wondering whether he should disturb her or not. Finally he walked slowly into the parlour, making no sound. He stopped in front of the couch where she rested, and she, not knowing who it was, was frightened almost out of her wits. Her eyes flew open, she gasped, and she could comprehend only that the light from the candle was blocked by a solid masculine shape. She did what anyone, frightened as she was, would have done. She screamed.

'Paige, Paige,' he said urgently, grasping her by the shoulders. She, fully awake now, realised that it was only Chad, and her fear subsided, but slowly. She sagged against him, almost collapsing. He knelt and held her in the circle of his arms, stunned by her unreasoning fear.

'I didn't mean to frighten you,' he soothed, his voice calm, steady, and free of the brusqueness that she had learned to expect from him.

The sherry had left her feeling a trifle dizzy.

'I—I——' She tried to speak, but her fright, along with the sherry, had left her tongue incapable of wrapping itself around words.

'Do you know where the flashlight is?'

'I—I'm not sure,' Paige said indistinctly, still shaking uncontrollably. 'I've left it somewhere.'

Chad sat down beside her, his brow wrinkling in sudden concern. 'Is anything wrong? You didn't get an electric shock, did you?'

She shook her head, trying to ignore her rapid heartbeat. 'Help me up and I'll look for the flashlight.'

'No, wait. You're still trembling,' he said. 'I can't imagine how I managed to scare you so. Look, I'm not a werewolf.' He held his hands towards her. 'See? No hair on my palms.' He smiled at her, trying to cheer her.

She appreciated his effort and attempted to smile

back, but it was too soon after the shock of her fright. 'It's only that I was nervous about being alone in the Manse,' she managed to say at last. 'Then when I saw you standing above me——'

'You thought I was a burglar.' The expression on his face softened. Then he had a sudden thought. 'Say, you're not getting sick, are you?'

He scrutinised her closely, taking in her pale face, seeing that she was still shivering. He lifted his hand up and put it to her forehead, letting it linger. 'You don't seem to have a fever,' he said, relieved.

Her skin tingled at his touch, and from the startled look in his eyes she could tell that he felt it too. Here they were, alone again, in a situation that she had sworn to herself would never recur. Chad, suddenly serious, ran a forefinger down the line of her cheekbone to her lips, traced their fullness, gently touched her chin, inclined her head towards his.

She couldn't believe that it was happening in spite of all her good intentions, but Chad's lips were upon hers, drinking in her kisses. And, as before, she felt herself responding with a lack of inhibition that only a few weeks ago would have been out of the question. And still would be, with anyone else.

Anyone else? All at once the idea of kissing anyone else seemed offensive. How had she come to this point? She had never tied herself down to one man, even at the height of her romance with Stephen. Now here she was thinking that she never wanted to kiss anyone but Chad Smith—and come to think of it, she knew no more about him, really, than she had in the beginning.

It was impossible to ignore his lips, nipping softly at her neck, his arms, strong and muscular and holding her close. She felt her breathing speed up, her heart beating wildly. She lifted her head and felt his tongue against the tender skin of her throat. She heard herself moan lightly with the sheer exquisite pleasure of it.

His expert hands slid beneath her loose smock, and

their heat suffused her and mingled with the glow from the sherry. Her breasts swelled with the sensation of warmth, their nipples rising to meet his eager fingers.

It wasn't possible, given the height of her arousal, for Chad to be unaware of it. As from a far distance, she saw his fingers working at the buttons of her smock, allowed him to lay back the folds of fabric to expose one perfect breast, its nipple firm and ready for his touch.

'Paige,' he said softly, and his pronunciation of her name expressed his wonder at her beauty, limned as she was in the glow from the candle on the mantel.

She was lost, and she knew it. Her lips parted of their own volition, seeking to be conquered by his. Gentle hands cupped her breasts, applying careful rhythmic pressure to achieve the most excruciating pleasure. Paige's back arched slowly in gentle invitation, an invitation that Chad seemed willing to accept. Her hands slipped around him and under his shirt, reciprocating the delightful play of his own hands on her fevered flesh.

A victim of her own smouldering passion, she barely knew it when she shrugged her shoulders lightly to relieve herself of the cumbersome smock. Then she was bare to his gaze, ready to begin the lovemaking that she wanted, no, *needed*, in order to free herself from the gnawing tension that Chad Smith had so readily aroused.

He allowed himself to touch her for only a moment, then, seeming to come to his senses, he leaned back and looked at her as she gazed back at him from under heavy lids.

'Talk about electricity,' he said, keeping his tone light, but with obvious effort. 'When we're together, the sparks fly.' He straightened, sat up, smoothed his hair.

'You mean——?'

'I mean I'm going to short-circuit this love scene right now—nothing's going to happen. I know what your conditions are, and I can't take advantage of you in your aunts' home; it wouldn't be right to repay their hospitality that way.' Despite his attempt at light repartee, he stared at her for a moment, his eyes burning with raw emotion; then, quickly, so that she was not entirely sure what she had seen in them, he turned away.

Wearily Paige pulled on her smock, ignoring the clamouring of her senses. She desired him; that was the blunt truth of it. She had no idea how she could reconcile her newly discovered sexuality with her long-held values. She was sure Chad wanted her as much as she wanted him. She wondered how long he could be expected to respect her belief, especially when her moral code seemed to fly out the window every time he touched her.

But now that he had made the break, she determined to bring their relationship back to a more casual footing immediately. 'I may have left the flashlight in the dining room,' she said, her words falling out in a rush. She stood a bit unsteadily, although her shakiness was not from fear or the lingering effect of the sherry. She was stone-cold sober now, and passion had driven out fear.

Chad led the way to the dining room, carrying the candle, and they found the flashlight. His inspection of the electric range was slow and deliberate. Finally he unplugged it from the electric outlet and went down into the basement for several minutes.

'I don't think you should use the range until I can find a qualified appliance repair man to come out here and look at it,' he said when he returned. 'We'll just leave it unplugged. But as far as I can tell, the electrical problem is confined to the range. The Manse's wiring seems all right.' He threw the master electric switch and the Manse blazed into light, which found them standing in the middle of the kitchen blinking at one another.

'I have a hot plate in the Sea House,' said Chad. 'We can use that for cooking until the range is repaired.'

'Fine,' said Paige. They stared at each other, his eyes hot upon her, then Chad switched off the flashlight and turned to leave by the kitchen door. He paused and looked back at her.

For a brief moment an unnamed emotion flickered over Chad's features and he looked as if he had something he wanted to say. But whatever it was, he didn't shape it into words. Instead he pivoted on his heel and walked out, and Paige, feeling suddenly, discouragingly, bereft, heard his footsteps retreating down the path as he disappeared into the forest.

CHAPTER SIX

CHAD was up and away from St Albans early, soon after dawn. He left a note tacked to the back door of the Manse. It was terse, almost abrupt. No salutation, no signature.

'Have gone to Brunswick to find repair man. You may use hot plate in Sea House.' That was all. Perhaps he was as eager to avoid her as she was to avoid him.

Oddly enough, she wasn't hungry in spite of the fact that she had skipped dinner last night. She toasted two slices of bread and ate them with butter and muscadine jelly, skipping coffee.

At lunchtime, seeing no sign of Chad, she wandered down to the dock and looked out across the green and blue expanse of the salt marsh. A cormorant, his feathers iridescent in the bright sunlight, paddled past, looking for a meal. He must have spotted a fish because he dived quickly, submerging, then rose to the surface several feet from the dock. He flew away, soaring towards the shore where he would eat his catch.

Paige saw no sign of Chad approaching in the *Marsh Mallow*, so after lingering for a few more moments she made her way back up the hill to the Manse. A methodical search of the refrigerator turned up only the oyster stew. She would like to eat it, but there was the problem of the hot plate. Well, Chad's note *had* said to use it, so perhaps she should walk down to the Sea House and heat her stew, maybe even eat it outside on the Sea House's front porch. She picked up the container of stew and set out, this time along the beach.

She opened the door to the Sea House carefully, curiously, feeling inhibited by an overwhelming feeling

Harlequin Romance

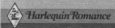
Harlequin Romance

MAN of Power
Mary Wibberley

Love Beyond Reason
Karen van der Zee

GET 4 BOOKS FREE

Harlequin Romance

The Winds of Winter
Sandra Field

The Leo Man
Rebecca Stratton

LOVE BEYOND REASON

There was a surprise in store for Amy!

Amy had thought nothing could be as perfect as the days she had shared with Vic Hoyt in New York City—before he took off for his Peace Corps assignment in Kenya.

Impulsively, Amy decided to follow. She was shocked to find Vic established in his new life. . .and interested in a new girl friend.

Amy faced a choice: be smart and go home. . .or stay and fight for the only man she would ever love.

MAN OF POWER

Sara took her role seriously

Although Sara had already planned her escape from the subservient position in which her father's death had placed her, Morgan Haldane's timely appearance had definitely made it easier.

All Morgan had asked in return was that she pose as his fiancée. He'd confessed to needing protection from his partner's wife, Louise, and the part of Sara's job proved easy.

But unfortunately for Sara's heart, Morgan hadn't told her about Monique. . .

Your Romantic Adventure Starts Here.

THE LEO MAN

"He's every bit as sexy as his father!"

Her grandmother thought that description would appeal to Rowan, but Rowan was determined to avoid any friendship with the arrogant James Fraser.

Aboard his luxury yacht, that wasn't easy. When they were all shipwrecked on a tropical island, it proved impossible.

And besides, if it weren't for James, none of them would be alive. Rowan was confused. Was it merely gratitude that she now felt for this strong and rugged man?

THE WINDS OF WINTER

She'd had so much— now she had nothing

Anne didn't dwell on it, but the pain was still with her—the double-edged pain of grief and rejection.

It had greatly altered her; Anne barely resembled the girl who four years earlier had left her husband, David. He probably wouldn't even recognize her—especially with another name.

Anne made up her mind. She just *had* to go to his house to discover if what she suspected was true. . .

These FOUR free Harlequin Romance novels allow you to enter the world of romance, love and desire. As a member of the Harlequin Home Subscription Plan, you can continue to experience all the moods of love. You'll be inspired by moments so real. . . so moving. . . you won't want them to end. So start your own Harlequin Romance adventure by returning the reply card below. <u>DO IT TODAY!</u>

NO POSTAGE
NECESSARY
IF MAILED
IN THE
UNITED STATES

BUSINESS REPLY CARD

First Class   Permit No. 70   Tempe, AZ

POSTAGE WILL BE PAID BY ADDRESSEE

Harlequin Reader Service
2504 W. Southern Avenue,
Tempe, Arizona 85282

that she didn't belong here. She quelled the feeling the best she could and looked around the room with interest. Last night the atmosphere had been so strained that she hadn't had a chance to see how Chad lived.

Chad's occupancy of the Sea House had transformed it from a simple rustic cottage with a magnificent view of the sea into a statement that revealed his own individuality. The rag rug above the fireplace, the stoneware jug filled with sea oats on the mantel, the rough texture of the wool serape that covered the bed— all combined to give an impression of a rugged man who travelled and who loved the natural tones and textures of the outdoors.

The room looked extremely neat, everything squarely in its place. The papers which had been scattered and stacked on the top of the library last night had been put away, probably in the low filing cabinet beside it. Out of curiosity Paige tried one of the doors; it refused to budge. Perhaps Chad had foreseen her inclination to snoop.

She browsed among the titles in the bookcase. Chad owned books of all kinds, but most of them concerned sailing. She recalled his annoyance when she had asked him about his sailboat. His annoyance seemed misplaced when she considered what she now deduced, from the contents of the bookshelves, as an avid interest in sailing. The callouses on his hands could very well have been caused by handling rigging, she supposed, and then she chided herself for being a poor detective. Callouses could be caused by any number of occupations—ditch digger, to name one. Only Chad Smith did not look like the type to be digging ditches.

Idly Paige picked up a large illustrated guidebook to France. Whenever her job required her to spend extra time in France, she loved to rent a car and roam the beautiful countryside. This book had excellent pictures, and to her surprise, it was written in French. Did Chad speak French, then, and could he read this book?

Nothing he had ever said or done had led her to believe that he was bi-lingual.

As she was thoughtfully closing the covers of the book, a Polaroid photograph slipped from between its pages. Paige caught it as it fell and moved closer to the window to look at it. It was a very bad picture of a trophy of some sort.

She turned the snapshot over, looking for a date or a name or an explanation. Nothing. She looked at it again, and noted that the object on top of the trophy was definitely a sailboat. The writing engraved on the base of the trophy was almost indecipherable due to the poor quality of the photo itself. She couldn't make out the year or much of anything else except, very faintly, the name Smith.

Carefully she replaced the snapshot in the guidebook. The few things she had discovered about Chad at least gave her something to think about, she thought as she went to the hot plate, which was located on a low table in the corner. Above it, in a small cupboard, she found a cook-and-serve pan in which she heated the oyster stew. It seemed clear that Chad was avidly interested in sailboats. Why, then, would he refuse to talk about *his* boat?

When the stew was hot, she poured it into an earthenware bowl and carried it outside where she sat on the stone steps and looked out over the ocean as she ate, mulling Chad Smith over in her mind. Unfortunately, she hadn't really turned up enough information to reach any definite conclusion about either Chad's origins or his intentions.

She finished, washed up in the tiny bathroom, and replaced the pan in the cupboard, then looked around the room once more, preparing to leave. She hesitated and went to stand at the window, admiring the sweep of the blue sea on three sides. Chad had left the windows uncurtained and the view was unimpeded.

She turned to leave, but her eyes fell on a sheaf of

papers that had fallen behind the wicker basket beside the door. She bent over to pick them up, noticed that they had become wrinkled, and started to flatten the top sheet with her hand. She could hardly help noticing the subject matter.

The top paper had to do with boats, something about rigging and sails. Sailboats, again. The second paper was a sketch of a racing yacht, complete down to the last detail. The third paper seemed to be a comparison of racing times. The other papers appeared to concern technical sailing data, all in Chad's handwriting.

Paige had just straightened the stack of papers when she dropped them. They scattered across the polished wood floor, and she had to get down on her hands and knees to pick them up.

She was in the process of retrieving one sheet that had fallen between the bed and the table beside it when she saw an envelope that had slipped down into the same crevice. She picked that up, too, when she saw that the logo in the top left-hand corner was that of the aunts' bank in Brunswick.

Turning the envelope over in her hand, she saw the note scribbled in pencil in Aunt Biz's sprawling hand. It only said, 'Chad—please handle,' but it filled her with alarm. Here was a clue of some sort, if only she could figure it out. It was a link between the aunts and Chad, a financial link.

Aunt Biz and Aunt Sophie and her late Uncle John had been left financially independent through a trust set up by their father before his death many years ago. Paige well remembered visits to Brunswick in the *Marsh Mallow* several times every summer with Aunt Biz, when they would walk to the bank and Aunt Biz would disappear into old Mr Lingfelt's office for a long consultation.

Afterwards Mr Lingfelt's secretary would give Paige a red lollipop and Mr Lingfelt would pat Paige on the head, and Aunt Biz, looking pleased, would leave the bank clutching a long white envelope and take Paige to the near-by drugstore soda fountain for a chocolate soda.

Aunt Biz had always handled the financial and business angles of their trust for the aunts and, when he was alive, Uncle John. She said that she enjoyed the adding and subtracting and determining where the money should go. In fact, that was why she had always been called Aunt Biz—Biz for her fine head for business, Uncle John had said.

So why was Aunt Biz turning over anything from her bank to Chad with a hastily scribbled note asking him to handle it for her?

She scrutinised the envelope carefully. It had a glassine window on the front, but it held nothing inside. It was the kind of envelope that might have once held a cheque or a bank statement, however. She sank down on Chad's bed, the wool serape rough against her bare legs, and wrinkled her forehead in thought. She could think of nothing that Aunt Biz could be turning over to Chad, unless perhaps it was a pay check, and Aunt Biz herself had told Paige that Chad received only room and board in exchange for his work on St Albans.

Finally, unable to make any sense out of it, she rose from Chad's bed and put the papers where he would see them in the middle of the long table. She held the envelope in her hand for a few minutes, puzzling over it. Then, walking quickly back to the bed, she bent over and shoved it back in the crevice between the bed and the table. At the moment, she would just as soon not let Chad know that she had seen it.

She walked back through the woods, immersed in thought. As she approached the Manse she heard the hum of a high-powered boat, and it sounded as though it were approaching the St Albans dock.

It couldn't possibly be Chad, not in a boat so powerful. Paige knew all too well the tinny chug-chug of the *Marsh Mallow*. Wondering, she ran down the path to the dock and saw a sleek powerboat being tied to a piling by a nice-looking dark-haired man who appeared to be a few years younger than Chad.

'Hi,' he said, before she could greet him. He jumped out on the dock and held out his hand. 'I'm Lee Tracy from Golden Isles Boating Center. How do you like your aunts' new boat?'

Paige was speechless. 'Their new boat? There must be some mistake!' The boat was a low-lying ChrisCraft with an inboard motor, long and sleek and white. The name lettered across the stern was *Paige One*.

'No mistake. Chad Smith said to tell you to sign for it.'

'I can't do that!' Paige was incredulous. 'My aunts told me nothing about a new boat, and I certainly can't guarantee that they'll pay for it.'

'You don't have to. The boat was bought in their name—see, it's right here—but it's already paid for.'

'And who paid for it?'

'Why, Chad Smith, of course. He had to go pick up an appliance repair man, that's why he's late, but he'll be here soon. He's going to give me a ride back to the mainland.'

Paige was flabbergasted, but she looked over the papers that Lee Tracy wanted her to sign and they didn't appear to obligate her or the aunts to anything; they merely stated that she had received delivery of the boat. With a shrug, she signed. Chad would have some explaining to do.

There was an awkward silence after she handed the signed papers back to Lee. Obviously he expected to be invited to the Manse; she could hardly leave him waiting alone on the dock for Chad, who might arrive in five minutes or in an hour.

'Would you like a glass of iced tea?' she asked at last, albeit reluctantly.

Lee Tracy smiled and nodded. He was really very attractive, she decided as he turned to follow her up the path. He was tall, though not as tall as Chad, and trim. He was deeply tanned and his hair was dark brown and windblown.

At the Manse Paige indicated a settee and two chairs grouped around a table in the side yard beside a cabbage palm tree. 'Do make yourself comfortable,' she said. 'I'll be back in just a minute.'

When she returned with the iced tea, garnished with a sprig of mint from Aunt Biz's garden, Lee was stretched out on the settee, looking relaxed and comfortable. He took the iced tea and regarded her with an admiring expression.

'So you're Biz and Sophie's niece.'

'Yes, here for a short visit.'

'How long will you stay?'

'A bit longer. My aunts are visiting in Macon, and I'll stay on for a while after their return. Do you live in Brunswick?'

Lee shook his head. 'I live on St Simons. I commute across the causeway to Brunswick to work every day; it's a fifteen-minute drive.'

'Have you ever thought of getting a job on St Simons? It's such a lovely island—you must hate to leave it every morning.'

'I do, but I won't be looking for a job closer to home. I own the Golden Isles Boating Center; we draw our customers from all of the sea islands, so Brunswick on the mainland is a perfect central location. How about you—what do you do for a living?'

She told him, and he seemed interested. He had vacationed in Paris last year, so she related several anecdotes about her experiences there. They were laughing together when they heard the approach of the *Marsh Mallow*.

In a few minutes Chad was striding up the path followed by a workman carrying a toolbox: the repair man. Chad waved briefly and took the man inside the Manse. He reappeared shortly carrying his own glass of iced tea, sat down in the chair opposite Paige and grinned at her the way he had during her first days on St Albans, before the physical side of their relationship had veered out of control.

'How do you like the new boat?' he asked.

'It's very nice,' she hedged, unwilling to make an issue of this unauthorised purchase in front of Lee.

He eyed her closely. 'Come on, what do you really think? What I see in your eyes isn't wholehearted approval. Surely you're not going to miss the old *Marsh Mallow*?'

'Of course not,' she said, much too sharply. Chad's eyes burned into her, and she was suddenly aware that he wanted her approval of his purchase of the boat. Well, he wouldn't get it, not until he could explain how he had paid for it, and maybe not even then.

Lee sensed the strained atmosphere between Paige and Chad and tried to make light of it by changing the subject. Chad sat, his eyes on Paige, not contributing or responding to Lee's efforts to include him. When the repair man emerged from the Manse, Chad excused himself and went inside for a conference with him, leaving Paige alone with Lee.

'Do you get over to the mainland often?' asked Lee when Chad had gone.

Paige shook her head. 'I haven't been off St Albans since I arrived,' she confessed, just now realising it. 'It's so lovely here that I——'

'Nonsense,' said Lee briskly. 'I agree that St Albans is beautiful, but you need to socialise once in a while. Why don't you have dinner with me tonight? I'll come back after work, pick you up in my boat, and we'll find a good restaurant.'

His invitation surprised her. 'Well——' she began.

'Don't make me twist your arm. And I should tell you that I'm a very good arm-twister.'

Paige laughed. 'All right, then. What time shall I be ready?'

'About half-past seven. Dress casually.'

They were interrupted by Chad and the repair man, who spoke to them briefly and went on down the path towards the dock, carrying his toolbox.

'It was just a minor problem with the range, something wrong with the burner,' Chad explained. 'Come on, Lee, I'll drop him off in Brunswick with you.'

Lee rose to leave, and Paige walked them both to the dock. The three men climbed into the new boat and cast off. Before Chad, who was at the wheel, turned towards Brunswick, Lee called out, 'See you later tonight, Paige.' He lifted a hand in farewell.

Chad sent her a quick searching glance and then examined Lee's expression. But when neither Lee nor Paige made any further comment, Chad tightened his lips and squinted into the sun, turning the boat in a spume of spray that glittered like so many falling diamonds. *Paige One* sped away with a swiftness unmatched by the poor old *Marsh Mallow* even in its salad days.

Casual dress, Lee had said, so after a shower she leafed through her closet until she found a full-skirted dress in cool aquamarine Indian cotton with matching lace at the keyhole neckline and at the hem. Her sandals, low-heeled, were the same colour, and, thinking about the effect of the wind in her hair during the boat ride from St Albans, she wound a cobalt blue scarf around her head for a turban effect. Gold seashell earrings completed the look. When she had dressed, she went to the veranda outside the study and stood leaning against one of the posts that supported the balcony above, looking out over the ocean.

She didn't hear Chad walking up behind her. His hands on her shoulders, slowly turning her to face him, were the first indication that he had returned from his boat trip to Brunswick.

He spoke tersely, clipping his words short. 'You have

a date with Lee tonight.' It was a statement, not a question.

Paige nodded, staring up at him, suddenly tongue-tied.

His light eyebrows knit together, his eyes pierced the thin veneer of her composure. In the distance she could hear the rise and fall of the sea and the cry of seagulls. She wondered if he could read her mind, if he knew that she didn't want to go out with Lee, not really.

But this was something she couldn't put into words because she knew where those words would lead—back to the uncontrollable passion that she had felt last night. For a moment she felt the ache of desire that his lovemaking had inspired, and she knew then that she didn't need his kisses or his caresses in order to desire him. All it took was a look from him, the blaze of his eyes on her face.

He spoke quietly, but his words carried weight. 'You know I'm fond of you, Paige.'

'Fond of me?' So amazed was she by his words that she could only repeat them, parrotlike.

'Yes, fond. As in like. As in caring. But this communion of spirit you're looking for has me confused. I'm waiting for you to tell me when you feel it. With me, I mean.'

Paige swallowed before she spoke, but then she raised her chin and looked him in the eye. Her words spilled out, one on top of the other. 'What I'm looking for is love and openness between two people, and yes, caring. But it's also trust, Chad. Trust. Think about that.'

With a sickening thud her mind fell back to the Sea House today when she had found the envelope that tied Chad to her aunts' financial dealings. How could she trust him as long as she didn't know who he was, what he was doing here? Especially when he didn't seem over-anxious to reveal anything about himself to her.

'Anything else?' He was looking at her strangely, and his voice was tinged with irony.

'Yes, there is something else. How did you buy that boat, Chad? That expensive boat that Lee delivered? And in my aunts' name, too? And who gave you permission to name the boat *Paige One*?' Her voice sounded tight and strained; she found herself willing Chad to give her a reasonable explanation for the purchase of the boat. She wanted her unresolved questions answered, and she wanted, more desperately than she had realised, to be able to believe in him.

'As for naming the boat after you, I thought you'd be pleased. Aunt Sophie and Aunt Biz will think that the name is highly original. And—and naming the boat *Paige One* has a special meaning for me, one which you couldn't possibly understand at the moment.'

'I understand one thing. You're taking too much into your own hands around here. Something isn't right.'

Chad sighed and walked a few steps away before turning to face her. 'Look, Paige, it's all perfectly legal. The important thing is that Aunt Sophie and Aunt Biz have a decent boat to travel back and forth to Brunswick and St Simons in. That old scow of theirs could barely make it to——'

'I know how awful the *Marsh Mallow* is. I agree that a new boat is necessary. But if you spent their money for a boat without their knowledge—and I can't believe they knew anything about a new boat when they left St Albans—how did you do it? By whose authority?'

'They didn't know they were getting a new boat when they left here, that's true. You'll agree that they'll be delighted with it, though, don't you?'

'Yes, but——'

'Don't worry about your aunts' money. I assure you that everything is under control.'

'But whose control?' retorted Paige unhappily. Her eyes searched his face for the least bit of reassurance, but she didn't find it. His expression was stony, impassive. Whatever his thoughts were, there was no way of reading them.

Chad didn't answer, and the air between them vibrated with unvoiced thoughts.

Paige turned on her heel and walked back into the Manse, her sandals clicking across the hardwood floor. They were at an impasse; there was nothing more to be said. If she was going to find out what was going on here, it apparently wouldn't be from Chad Smith.

The drone of an approaching motorboat heralded Lee's arrival. Paige picked her handbag up off the hall table and walked swiftly down to the dock to meet him. The exchange with Chad had unnerved her, and all she wanted was to get away from him. Away from him and St Albans and the worry about her aunts' affairs that was threatening to become almost constant.

After a quick boat journey to Lee's house on St Simons and a short drive through the village, Lee suggested dinner at a restaurant on the ocean. Inside it was dimly lit and informal with high wide uncurtained plate-glass windows that included the Atlantic Ocean in the restaurant's décor. Lee asked for a table beside the window, and the waiter led them to a corner table beneath an unusual macramé wall hanging knotted in blue and green swirls depicting the movement of ocean waves. It was not lost on Paige that Lee thoughtfully contrived to seat her in the chair with the best view of the moon upon the ocean.

When they had ordered, Lee leaned across the table.

'So tell me more about yourself,' he prompted. 'You work for an airline, you travel to Paris. That's all I know about you, and it isn't nearly enough.'

Paige smiled. 'And what else would you like to know?'

'What you do in your spare time, what are your favourite foods, colours, flowers, and how you happened to come to St Albans—for a start. And then after that, we can move on to——'

'Wait a minute!' protested Paige. 'You're getting ahead of me. In my spare time I read or sketch or design and work needlepoint. I like Chinese food and French food and plain old Southern cooking, my favourite colour is green in any shade, and I'm wild about daffodils. And I came to St Albans to visit my aunts, because when I heard about——' and then she bit her lip, realising that she had been about to reveal her real reason for visiting.

'When you heard about what?' Lee raised his eyebrows at her.

Despite her urge to confide her fears to someone, anyone, Paige decided for now that it would be best to keep her own counsel. 'I—I was concerned when I learned that they'd arranged for Chad to live on the island with them,' she said carefully.

'Oh, I see. You were afraid that the old girls might be in need of more help than they would admit, so you decided to come and see how well they were really getting along. Well, you must be reassured. I've never seen two more self-sufficient women, and I know people twenty years their junior who don't have as much energy.'

'Yes,' said Paige, cautiously deciding to leave it at that. If Lee Tracy wanted to think she was only concerned about her aunts' ability to live alone on the island, she would let him.

Fortunately, their food arrived at that moment and provided a welcome break in the conversation.

Paige concentrated on her dinner, a platter of succulent golden-fried shrimp. Their talk while they ate touched on various subjects, including Lee's business, the recent development of St Simons Island into a resort area, and the delicious almond muffins that the restaurant served with dinner. The time passed quickly, and all too soon they were finished.

Afterwards, they walked slowly along the boardwalk that separated the restaurant from the ocean, letting the soft sea breeze blow across their faces. Paige's skirt fluttered in the wind; she walked carefully so that her heels would not catch in the gaps between the boards.

When the wind grew stronger, Lee said, 'I think we'd better end our walk.' He cast a watchful eye at the sky, where wisps of clouds scudded across the face of the moon. 'It looks as though I should get you back to St Albans.'

'Why? Do you think there's a tropical storm out there?'

'I haven't heard of one. But if the wind gets any stronger, it won't be safe to make the trip back to the island. We'd better go.'

Their boat trip back to St Albans was uneventful, despite the rising winds.

'I enjoyed our evening together,' said Lee when they had reached the Manse, and Paige turned to face him in the glare of the overhead porch light.

'So did I,' she replied. He might have kissed her then, but before he could make a move, she put out her hand. 'Thank you,' she said, rather formally.

'You don't have a telephone, so I can't call you. But perhaps I'll see you again.' Lee's voice was smooth; he held her hand firmly in his.

She should have said 'I hope so,' or, 'That would be lovely.' But somehow she couldn't say the words, she simply didn't have the heart for them. And there was no point in leading him on if she didn't really want to see him again. So she only smiled and said, 'Goodnight,' then she slipped quickly inside the door before he could say anything else.

She went slowly to her room, lost in thought. If only she had responded to Lee more than she had, if only she had felt something more for him than mild interest. He could provide an antidote to Chad Smith, the diversion that she needed to get Chad out of her system. For, she was rapidly discovering, Chad had become something more than an enigma to her. He had become a compulsion. Paige hated to admit it, even to herself, but it was true. Why else did she think about him even when she was with a man who was almost equally attractive? Why else did his face keep intruding into her consciousness, his rugged face with its strong profile, his lips so disturbingly sensual, his eyes so compelling?

She reached the top of the stairs and closed her eyes, clinging to the banister with one hand. She willed herself to erase his face from that place in her head where it had impressed itself, but it wouldn't go away. It stayed there, part of her consciousness, tormenting her with unanswered questions, the answers to which would tell her who he was and what he was doing here.

She wished she had never had occasion to get involved with someone whose background was so sketchy and incomplete; she hated the thought that Chad Smith might turn out to be entirely disreputable. So far, he had certainly done nothing to win her confidence. But then why should he? He had the wholehearted approval of both her aunts.

Paige sighed and went into her room, closing the door behind her. She took off her dress, hung it in the closet, and slipped her sheerest nightgown over her head. She was tired, but it was not a physical weariness. She was finally beginning to show the strain of her agonising uncertainty about the situation on St Albans. One thing was clear to her: if she were to be of any use to the aunts, she would have to find out once and for all who Chad Smith was. And once the aunts returned, her opportunity for checking into his background would be drastically reduced. She would have to do her sleuthing quietly, unobtrusively, and she would have to do it now, while they were still in Macon. Paige had seen enough of her aunts' over-protectiveness where Chad was concerned to know that if they suspected that she was intruding on Chad's privacy, they would be highly indignant and might even hamper her efforts to find out as much as she could.

Brushing her hair before the cheval mirror beside the long French doors, she came to a decision. She *would* find out more about Chad Smith, no matter how much she personally dreaded finding out the truth. She would use whatever means she could to check on his background, to find out why he had in his possession an envelope from her aunts' bank with a scribbled message from Aunt Biz.

And when she found out what he was up to, when she had discovered his secret, she would confront him with what she knew. In the process, perhaps she would even exorcise his unfathomable hold on her emotions and his bewildering power to unleash the passion that she found so utterly disturbing.

When she had brushed her hair until it rippled softly around her shoulders, she walked to the low dressing-table to put away her brush. As she passed in front of the French doors, she realised that the wind from the sea had become stronger, and she thought she heard the slamming of a shutter against the house.

With an impatient sigh, she ran lightly downstairs and to the study, where she wrenched open the French doors and stood indecisively on the veranda, scanning the row of windows that opened on to it. Sure enough, the shutter on the end window was flapping in the wind, banging noisily against the house. Paige walked swiftly to secure it, noting that rain had begun to fall and was being whipped across the corner of the veranda by the wind.

The recalcitrant shutter refused to be bolted in place; she would no sooner force it back against the wall than a puff of wind would sweep around the corner of the house and tear it from her grasp. Her nightgown was getting soaked, and her hair was beginning to cling damply to her neck. She wished she had just let the shutter flap; it didn't seem as though she was going to be able to conquer it.

Someone ran past the veranda, splashing through puddles, holding a raincoat over his head. It was Chad, of course. He saw her trying to fasten the shutter and said, 'Paige! Let me do that. I noticed that it was loose the other day when I was painting the trim out here, and I meant to repair it before the next storm.' He dropped the raincoat and grasped the shutter, adding his strength to hers to push it against the house. This time, the bolt clicked into place.

'There,' he said, somewhat out of breath. For the first time he looked at her. Paige stepped away from him, wishing she had thought to throw on a robe over her transparent gown, now wet and clinging to the ripe contours of her body.

'Paige,' he said, this time quietly, a despairing note to his voice. His eyes, glowing with a light of their own, embraced her, taking in the seductive outline of her breasts, plainly visible under her clinging gown, and the slim lines of her waist, swelling into the smooth curves of her hips.

She turned to run, her loose hair flinging water droplets at him, but before she could put any distance between them, his big hand grasped her roughly by her upper arm, almost bruising her with unaccustomed brute force.

'Wait,' he said hoarsely, twisting her around to face him, pinning her against the wall. 'I can't let you go. Not until——' and his lips devastated hers in a torrent of passion. With a surge of despairing joy, she let him revel in her kisses, returning desire with beautiful, mystical desire.

With the rain whirling around them, drenching them, lending its sea-sweet flavour to their kisses, Paige felt totally unlike herself. She was someone else tonight, a rainborne spirit flying on the wind to heights of which she had never even dreamed. She clasped Chad to her, feeling the strong, solid bulk of him pressed tightly to the most sensitive parts of her, clinging with an unfamiliar lightheaded euphoria to his body, the only thing that seemed to link her with the solid ground of ordinary earthbound mortals.

He released her lips with a low moan and buried his

face in her damp hair, caressing the tender spot at the base of her throat with his gentle lips, breathing his warm breath on her rain-slick skin.

She felt herself bending backwards, felt her loose hair clinging to her back, felt his lips warm upon her breast through the flimsy gown.

Suddenly a sharp bolt of lightning stabbed through the sky, followed by an almost instantaneous crash of thunder from the direction of the sea. Its echoes reverberated over the island, vibrating the veranda, bringing Paige to her senses. Another bolt of lightning followed fast upon the first, flashing its blue-white light across their startled faces.

It was no longer safe to remain on the veranda. Chad's hands released their grasp on her, and she backed away from him, holding his eyes with her own, knowing that if she held his eyes for one more moment, one more eternity, she would have no choice but to allow herself to submit to him despite all the perfectly good reasons not to.

Hot and brilliant, his eyes returned her gaze. When he spoke, it was with a fevered passion and an intensity that left no doubt that he wanted her as much as she wanted him. 'I'll tell you this: don't think it's easy for me, Paige.' His eyes, searching her face, held a mute plea that she didn't understand. In fact, it seemed to her that she didn't understand anything any more. A sob of frustration pushed itself up from somewhere inside her, and she turned and fled swiftly into the Manse, away from Chad Smith.

In her room, she ran to the open doors across the length of the balcony and slammed them shut, one by one. When she reached the last one, something made her look out into the rainy night, and she saw Chad, standing in the rain, water glittering on his skin in the light from the door where she stood.

He stood as though transfixed, his eyes raised to her as she stood above him. For a breathless moment their eyes caught and held, green upon amber, and then slowly as she watched, Chad melted into the rain and was gone.

Paige backed away from the balcony railing, gripped the doorframe, stumbled blindly inside and slammed the door against the night and against Chad Smith. She could feel her heart pounding unreasonably, felt her breath coming in little gasps. All because he had held her in his arms and kissed her into a magical, mystical haze, all because she had looked into his rain-veiled eyes, all because he had a hold on her that she was helpless to explain. She was inexplicably drawn to him in a way that brooked no resistance, and having had no experience whatsoever with this overpowering sense of physical attraction, she knew nothing about how to deal with it. Finally, fitfully, she fell asleep, a welcome sleep that gave her a few hours' respite from the picture of Chad Smith that intruded into every aspect of her consciousness.

CHAPTER SEVEN

THE whir of the helicopter's rotor blades woke her abruptly the next morning. For a moment she thought it was still night-time and that the unfamiliar noise was somehow connected with the storm, but then she became conscious of the muted sunbeams filtering through the curtained French doors. She slipped from her bed and padded across the floor to investigate.

The helicopter was hovering over the level section of the lawn just in front of the place where it began to slope towards the the beach.

'Why, it's landing here!' she exclaimed out loud to herself in surprise. Quickly she ran to the closet and pulled on a pair of white jeans and an apricot-coloured polo shirt. She briefly raked her hairbrush through her hair and brushed her teeth. There was barely time for lipstick, and then she skipped downstairs two steps at a time. She couldn't imagine what had brought a helicopter to St Albans, unless it was some sort of emergency. Her throat contracted. If anything had happened to the aunts . . .

The rotors were slowing to a stop just as she stepped out on the downstairs veranda. A long-legged figure with black curly hair thrust the helicopter door open and climbed out. He closed the door behind him and turned towards her, smiling.

'Stephen!' she exclaimed. There was no mistaking who it was. She had never seen him wearing this blue jumpsuit before; the deep shade of blue made his eyes seem even bluer than she remembered.

'You've certainly managed to hide yourself away very effectively,' he observed, striding towards her with long steps. His eyes held the bright gleam of possession in their dazzling blue depths.

'How did you find me?' Paige was thunderstruck to see him here.

'It wasn't easy,' he said. He stood looking down at her, devouring her with his eyes. 'How have you been?'

'What are you doing here?'

'Aren't you going to invite me in? We both seem to be asking questions, and no one's answering them.' He grinned down at her, pleased that he had surprised her.

'I didn't know you were coming,' she said helplessly, sensing that he had stopped just short of kissing her. Before he seized the opportunity, she turned quickly to go inside the Manse.

'It's not as though I could telephone,' he pointed out as he followed her, taking in the spacious study, the books carefully dusted by Paige, the brass doorknobs now restored to their former shine.

Paige took a deep breath and turned to face him. 'Didn't you get my letter?' she asked him.

'Of course I got your letter—that's why I'm here. You can't possibly think that I'd let you go so easily. What kind of way was that to tell me it's all over, anyway?'

She could hardly believe that he had travelled the nine hundred miles from New York to demand an explanation, and she wasn't prepared to give one. She opened her mouth to speak, then closed it again.

Stephen shook his head. 'I'm still asking questions, and no one's answering them. Look, I'm not leaving here until you talk about this with me. Why don't you offer me a cup of coffee?'

'Stephen, I——'

'I haven't eaten anything this morning, and you know I hate to fly on an empty stomach. I can't concentrate when I'm weak from hunger. Imagine how awful you'd feel if I had to ditch the 'copter in the marsh on the way back to Brunswick. Show me to the kitchen, that's a good girl.'

Paige had never liked Stephen's bossiness, but it looked as though she would never get rid of him unless she could convince him that their romance, if indeed it had been that, was over, truly over. She sighed and said, 'Follow me. I suppose I can find some bacon and eggs.'

Stephen sat at the kitchen table, watching her as she scrambled the eggs.

'Quite a place your aunts have here,' he remarked cheerfully.

'The island has been in my family for generations,' she told him.

'It's a godforsaken place,' he said. 'I'll bet the mosquitoes are terrible. I can't imagine why anyone would want to live here.'

Paige shot him a long look and decided he meant it. She shrugged off the remark; it wasn't worth her time to try to tell him how much the island and its beauty meant to her. Stephen had never appreciated aesthetic things; to him, life was a path to run along pell-mell, never mind smelling the rosebuds along the way.

The bacon sizzled in the pan, filling the kitchen with its aroma. 'I didn't know you could fly a helicopter,' she said, changing the subject.

'I learned when I was in the service.'

'You're taking a few days off from your job?'

'Just my regular time off. I had to see you, Paige. What happened between us?'

Paige set the eggs and bacon down in front of him and poured them each a cup of coffee. *Exactly nothing*, she thought to herself, thinking of the overpowering physical attraction she felt for Chad. Nothing like it had ever affected her when she was with Stephen.

She sat down across from him and let her eyes meet his. She was looking at an undeniably attractive man, but he meant nothing to her at all. Her heart lifted. She had made the right choice, telling Stephen that they

were through. And now it looked as though she would
have to justify it.

But not yet. She heard the familiar stomp of feet at
the back door, and before she could call out to him,
Chad had thrown the door open and was standing there
staring at them.

'I was going to ask you if you knew there was a
helicopter illegally parked on your front lawn, but——'

'It's all right, Chad,' Paige said quickly. Introductions
had to be made, so she got them over with as rapidly as
she could. 'Stephen McCall, this is Chad Smith.'

The two men took each other's measure, Chad
flicking his eyes over Stephen's trim blue jumpsuit.
Stephen took a bit longer with his assessment of Chad,
and Paige could see why. Today, knowing that he was
going to paint the upstairs hall, Chad had donned old
blue jeans, almost worn through at the seat and with
the ravelled legs cut off at two different lengths. They
were spotted with vari-coloured paint stains and were
possibly the most disreputable pair of pants that Paige
had ever seen. He also wore a tee-shirt that had once
been white, but was now similarly spotted and torn on
the sleeve where Chad had brushed against a
protruding nail. To top it off, he wore a sailor hat that
might have once belonged to the Ancient Mariner, so
tattered it had become. He had turned the brim down
low to protect his hair from the paint.

Some explanation seemed necessary. 'Stephen just—
er—dropped in to say hello,' she said, trying to make
light of his presence.

Chad raised his eyebrows to acknowledge her
attempt at wit, but Stephen seemed not to notice it.
'Nice to meet you,' Stephen said quickly, seriously.
While the two men were shaking hands, Paige saw the
light dawn in Chad's eyes. He was connecting Stephen
with the letters. If she hadn't been watching for it, she
never would have caught the brief shadow that passed
over Chad's face.

It seemed like a good idea to dispense with Chad immediately so that she could better deal with Stephen. 'Chad's going to paint the upstairs hall today,' she announced brightly to Stephen. 'He's my aunts' handyman.'

Chad slid her a look out of the corners of his eyes. 'That's right,' he said in a slow drawl. Paige stared at him. Picking up on her astonishment, he turned towards her and touched his hand to the brim of his hat. 'I'll get started on that hall right away, ma'am, soon as I bring in the ladder.'

Paige stifled a grin. She might have known that Chad would pull something like this! With a bob of his head, Chad turned and unceremoniously clumped down the porch stairs.

'Seems like a nice fellow,' observed Stephen a bit uncertainly.

'Oh, yes,' agreed Paige, hoping Chad was still within earshot. 'He's been a great help to my aunts.'

'I'm sure I've never met him before, but there's something so familiar about him.' Stephen looked puzzled. Then he shrugged. 'Well, I see a lot of people in a lot of places. I suppose he just reminds me of someone. Anyway, I want to talk about us. Paige——'

They were interrupted by a clattering on the porch. It was Chad with the ladder, and he fumbled with the door until Stephen, barely concealing his irritation at another interruption, got up to hold the door open. Chad trekked into the kitchen. 'Thanks,' he called back to Stephen, turning slightly. Whether it was by accident or design, Paige never knew, but the end of the ladder swung around and dashed Stephen's plate, still half-filled with scrambled eggs, on to the floor.

'Oh, sorry,' said Chad, a befuddled expression sliding over his face.

Paige glared at him. If he chose to act the fool, that was one thing, but now she'd have to clean up this mess.

'That's all right, Chad,' she said, struggling to keep her tone even. She didn't know whether to laugh or to erupt in anger.

'I'll get to the painting now,' he said, avoiding Paige's eyes, and he tramped through the downstairs hall and up the narrow stairs, whistling in that irritating manner of his.

Paige scooped the eggs into a dustpan and dumped them into the garbage. 'I'll scramble more eggs,' she said.

'No,' said Stephen. 'I want to talk with you.' He stood beside her; now he grasped her by the upper arms and turned her to face him.

She wouldn't look at him at first, not until he tilted her face up.

'Your letter surprised me,' he told her. 'I thought you'd decide to move into my apartment.'

Paige pulled away from him. 'No. I'm not ready for that kind of arrangement—it goes against everything I've ever believed.'

'I don't think you're thinking clearly.'

She shook her head. 'You might as well leave. We don't have anything further to discuss. You're asking for more than I can give.' She turned and walked through the hall and into the study, prepared to tell him goodbye.

Stephen followed and took her into his arms again. 'I'm not leaving yet. Don't pass this up, Paige. Come back to New York with me. Now.'

She wrenched away. Stephen seemed unwilling to take no for an answer. 'I'm simply not willing to live with you in unmarried bliss,' she said with what she hoped was cold finality.

'So what is it you want—a ring on your finger and a certificate that says you're Mrs Stephen McCall?' He spoke harshly.

'I don't want anything from you,' she cried. 'Leave me alone. Go back to New York and find someone else!'

Silence was heavy in the air.

'Do you mean that? Really?'

Paige studied him. There was no other possible answer. 'Yes, I mean it,' she whispered.

Stephen shook his head. 'You don't. I tell you, Paige, I want you to think about this carefully. I'm staying here until tomorrow morning, like it or not.'

'Stephen, you can't!' She was shocked to see the bold determination in his eyes.

'I won't force you to agree to anything. But I'm not leaving until tomorrow. There must be plenty of room in this old place. If you won't let me sleep in a bed, I'll spread a blanket on the veranda.' He stalked over to the couch and sat down, folding his arms over his chest as if to emphasise his immovability.

'Stephen——'

''Scuse me, ma'am, but what part of the hall did you want painted first? The part at the head of the stairs? Or should I start at Aunt Sophie's room?'

Paige whirled to see a subservient Chad Smith grinning at her like a sly jack-o'-lantern. Despite the problem of Stephen's stubborn presence on the couch, she almost burst out laughing.

'Paint the hall outside Aunt Sophie's room first,' she ordered, playing the role assigned to her with as much dignity as she could muster.

'Yes, ma'am,' he said, touching the brim of his hat and winking broadly at her before shuffling away.

She turned to deal with Stephen, who was sitting and scowling at her. Paige put her hands on her hips, looking down at him in exasperation, well aware that Chad could probably hear every word that was said, and not caring if he did.

'I'm not leaving,' said Stephen. 'I'll give you twenty-four hours to think about it. Then, if you still won't get in that helicopter with me, I'll go. And I daresay you'll never see me again, unless our paths cross at work.'

He meant what he said, and there seemed to be no budging him.

'Well, what do you mean to do? Camp out here in the study?'

'I won't make a nuisance of myself. Just go on about your business, doing what you usually do. You need time to think. I'll explore the island to keep busy.'

'I—I have some sewing I can do upstairs,' she said uncertainly. Really, this was the strangest situation!

'Go ahead.' Stephen stood up, shot her a too-confident smile, and walked swiftly out the door and towards the beach.

Paige closed her eyes and leaned against a near-by bookcase. Even though it was early morning, she felt unbelievably weary. Then she roused herself and stumbled upstairs. She actually did have sewing she could do, and it would keep her mind off the presence of Stephen.

When she reached the upstairs hall, Chad was just climbing down from the ladder, which was blocking the door to her room.

'Is your boy-friend leaving?' he asked. He was looking at her with the respect of a man who had been forced by circumstances to acknowledge the fact that she was attractive to other men.

'He's not my boy-friend.'

'He seems to think he is.'

Paige shrugged in exasperation. 'I wrote him and told him it was over.'

'And I mailed the letter, didn't I?' Chad's eyes bored into her.

'Yes, of course. Would you mind moving that ladder aside?'

'At least I did *something* to help you out,' said Chad, almost bitterly.

'That's more than I can say for this morning. You acted like a country bumpkin.'

'Who knows? Maybe I am.' Chad's eyes held a

challenge, despite his light tone. She felt as though he was mocking her for not knowing his true identity.

'Look, Chad, I'm really tired and I have sewing to do. Please let me in my room.'

Without a word, Chad slid the ladder aside. She could feel his eyes upon her back as she quickly went inside her room and closed the door.

She stood for a moment, looking out at the helicopter on the lawn. There was no sign of Stephen.

As she slip-stitched ball fringe along the edges of the powder-room curtains, she found herself becoming more and more depressed. She knew she wasn't going to change her mind about moving in with Stephen, and it was going to be difficult to get rid of him tomorrow morning without an explanation.

What if he refused to go, even after she had again told him that their relationship was over? She could ask Chad to force him to leave, but asking for Chad's help in such a situation would be demeaning to her. And she could hardly imagine a scene where Chad threw Stephen into his helicopter and ordered him off the island; such a scene would be ludicrous to say the least.

Paige tossed her sewing aside. Suddenly she felt confined, sitting alone in this room with the door closed. Chad was whistling outside her door as he painted, and his whistling had always irritated her. Restlessly she got up and went to the French doors. Stephen was not in evidence, but she knew she didn't want to risk running into him if she went outside the Manse.

If only she could get off the island for a time; if only she could run the new boat. She knew about the old *Marsh Mallow*, of course; one simply pulled the rope and if one was lucky, the motor started. But she had absolutely no desire to find herself stranded in the marsh when the unreliable motor conked out. She heard Chad move the ladder outside her bedroom door, and then his whistling stopped. His footsteps retreated down the stairs. He was probably taking a lunch break. This would be as good a time as any for her to leave her room. Paige gathered up her sewing and folded it in a drawer before tiptoeing out into the hall.

There was no sign of Chad in the kitchen, so she ate a quick lunch. She spared a brief thought for Stephen and his meal arrangements; well, he was welcome to rummage in the refrigerator and find something to eat, and knowing Stephen, she knew he would look after himself.

She headed for the boat dock and *Paige One*. Once she learned how to run the new boat, she would no longer be confined to the island. She could, at the first opportunity, go alone to Brunswick to see what she could find out about Chad.

Unavoidably, her thoughts reeled back to last night. Thinking about their damp encounter on the rainy veranda, it seemed almost as though Chad had cast a spell on her. How else could she explain her impassioned behaviour, which viewed more dispassionately today seemed nothing less than demented?

The *Paige One* rocked gently at the edge of the old dock, protected by a green canvas tarpaulin. Paige leaned over and pulled the tarpaulin aside. When she jumped aboard, her heart sank. The control panel was a mass of dials and switches and levers. Steering, she knew, was handled with a wheel much like steering wheels on automobiles. Other than that, she was totally unfamiliar with what she would have to know to get this boat started.

While she was engrossed in studying the controls, she heard a shouted greeting. She looked up and was startled, then dismayed, to see Chad walking down the path towards her.

'Looking over the new boat?' His attitude was genial; he had abandoned his clumsy handyman image, and he had showered and changed. He now wore a cocoa-brown shirt unbuttoned to mid-chest and a pair of spotless wheat-coloured jeans.

'I must say that you're looking much more civilized,' she commented.

Chad threw his head back and laughed. 'Do you think I fooled him? I was just providing a bit of levity for the situation. The two of you were getting much too serious.'

'*He* was getting serious, not I,' insisted Paige quickly.

'Yes, I know,' Chad replied, joining her in the boat. 'It's amazing how well voices carry in these high-ceilinged old houses.'

He flipped a few of the control-panel switches experimentally, and Paige wished impatiently that he would go away. She couldn't possibly figure out how to start the boat with Chad here; she'd have to leave and come back later when she had *Paige One* to herself.

'Say,' Chad said suddenly, 'want to go for a ride in her? I've been wanting to go over to Sea Island. There's a stable there and the attendant lets me exercise the horses sometimes; do you ride?'

Surprised at the invitation, she said, 'Yes, but——'

'Good, then it's settled. I'm tired of all this painting and hammering and—well, I want to do something different for a change.' His eyes rested on her appealingly.

It was hard to deny Chad anything when he was in this expansive mood; it was a complete relief from his former attitude of withdrawal and remoteness. Also, going with him would accomplish a purpose: it would get her away from Stephen. Besides, by watching Chad closely, she might be able to learn how to run the boat. That was what finally decided her.

'I'd love to go riding,' she said.

Chad began to loosen the lines that tied the ChrisCraft to the dock. 'Wait,' said Paige. 'Shouldn't I change?'

Chad ran his eyes over her figure, taking in the tight-fitting jeans, the light cotton shirt. 'No, it won't be necessary. You can ride in what you're wearing.' She sat down in the passenger seat, paying attention to what he was doing.

It looked very easy, she thought to herself as the powerful inboard motor roared into action. The levers and dials weren't at all mysterious after one saw them in use. Chad handled the boat masterfully, easing it away from the dock and then heading around the western tip of Little St Simons Island. As the island disappeared behind Little St Simons, Paige looked back once. She saw Stephen, who had evidently been drawn towards the sound of the boat motor, staring after them in perplexity, standing alone on the dock. She suppressed a smile at the consternation on his face. Chad noticed him too, reacting with an expression of smug satisfaction.

Paige recognised the tidal channel that the boat followed between St Simons and Sea Island; she had come this way often with Uncle John or Aunt Biz in the old days. Chad seemed practised in his navigation of the web of channels that threaded through the marshes. She ventured a glance at him, and he favoured her with a grin. Their unspoken conspiracy against Stephen, although entered into for two entirely different reasons, formed a bond between them.

Chad gestured towards the golden marsh grass, spread out before them like a brightly textured carpet. 'Beautiful, isn't it?' he enthused. 'The marshes of Glynn.'

'What did you call them?' Chad's remark momentarily caught her off balance, thinking as she was of leaving Stephen behind.

'The marshes of Glynn. Surely you studied the poet Sidney Lanier in school.'

Paige had to think for a moment. Then she recalled the Southern poet's masterpiece, *The Marshes of Glynn*; somehow she had forgotten that the long poem had been written when Sidney Lanier had been recovering from an illness here in Glynn County on the Georgia coast and had been influenced by the haunting beauty of the dense forests and the golden salt marshes.

Paige let her eyes rest on the marsh as the boat slowly twined its way along the narrow blue channel of water between the wide swathes of grass on either side, with Sea Island on one side and St Simons on the other. Beyond the marsh, on the dry land of the islands, grew the luxuriance of plant life nurtured by the semi-tropical climate. The gentle climate alone was enough to make the Golden Isles a favourite haven for tourists, many of whom returned later to take up residence.

Some of them chose St Simons, where new houses had been built to accommodate them. The wealthy, of course, lived in exclusive Sea Island's residential colony. Here, off a road flanked by ancient moss-draped oak trees, were the gracious and elaborate residential estates that contributed to Sea Island's image as a home for the élite.

But today, approaching by boat, they weren't going to see the big homes and beautifully landscaped lawns and gardens. Chad ran the boat up to a small dock, not in much better repair than the one at St Albans.

He helped Paige out of the boat; she looked about her curiously. There was a sand path that led up the bank from the water, but beyond that she saw only a tangle of undergrowth. Chad took the lead on the path and she followed him.

Chad was right; the stable was not far. Ahead she could see the low building with its brown roof.

The stable seemed deserted. Chad walked straight into the building without hesitation, calling out a greeting. A wizened man with a currycomb in his hand emerged from one of the stalls and removed his cap. 'Why, Chad,' he said. 'Going for a ride?' Paige was puzzled by the stable attendant's deferential manner.

'Yes, my friend and I want to take the horses out.'

'Good,' said the little man. 'I'll help you saddle them.'

'No, I want to do it,' Chad insisted. Paige followed him to the two end stalls where he stopped and patted the neck of a beautiful roan gelding and then went into the other stall where she could hear him talking softly to a big bay.

Chad turned when she approached the door to the stall. 'This is Damien,' he told her. Paige, whose eyes had quickly adjusted to the dim light in the stall, regarded the bay with respect. He was an extremely handsome gelding, sleek and well-groomed, and, if she was any judge of horseflesh, he was no ordinary stable hack. She put out a hand and touched him lightly on the neck. Damien whickered softly and nodded his head.

'He likes you,' said Chad. 'But he's a lot of horse. I think you'd be better off on Max.' They went into the other stall. Paige had expected Max to be somehow less impressive than Damien, but he showed fine breeding as well. Chad produced a sugar lump, and Paige held it out to Max. His soft nose nuzzled her hand.

Chad saddled the two horses quickly and competently, then led them out into the sunny paddock. He held Max while Paige mounted him, then vaulted into Damien's saddle. They urged the horses into a trot, Damien in front and Max following behind.

'There are miles of trails,' Chad called back over his shoulder. 'Some of them are really remote.'

Paige had no doubt of this; it seemed as though they were miles from civilisation already. Here, as on St Albans, grew enormous live oak trees fringed with grey Spanish moss. Farther on they passed clumps of holly and junipers, and they saw several tall magnolia trees bursting into bloom with big white blossoms. A squirrel chattered at them from a hole in a hollow tree, and a cardinal, bright red in a shaft of sunlight, regarded them warily from the branch of a pine tree.

Max proved to be an amiable mount; he had a sensitive mouth and responded readily to Paige's commands. With Chad on Damien in front of her, she could hardly ignore how well he sat a horse. Fine horsemanship was an art, Paige knew, a delicate balance of rider in communication with horse. She sensed this communication between Chad and Damien; it was unexpected. Watching Chad as he spoke quietly to the horse, she was surprised at the unity the two seemed to have achieved.

They rode for a time in silence until the trail where they rode passed close to a bluff overlooking the marsh. Chad half-turned in his saddle and said, 'Let's stop for a while, okay?'

Chad had chosen a peaceful place far from the stable. The marsh stretched away in front of them for miles, green and gold embracing the breathtaking blue of the sky. The hot afternoon sun beat down upon the scene, spangling the water between the reeds with shimmering pinpoints of light. As they watched, a big osprey, head and feet down, launched into a dive that ended in a plunge into the water. He vanished for a moment in the spray, then reappeared with a fish in his talons. He flew away across the marsh, winging homeward where he would divide his prey with his mate and young.

Chad watched this drama without comment. He motioned for Paige to sit down on a smooth flat rock, and when she did, he joined her. They sat in companionable silence, not needing to talk.

She was amazed at the easiness of their response to one another. For once she didn't feel that Chad was being aggressive, for once the overwhelming physical attraction that had dominated their relationship for so long seemed secondary to their feeling of comradeship. She wondered why, and decided it was the relaxed mood that they had attained here, away from the island. She had always felt that the isolated atmosphere on St Albans tended to intensify emotions; if she and Chad were any indication, it was true.

Chad had plucked a wild daisy from a clump within

arm's reach, and he began to tear off the petals. 'She loves me, she loves me not,' he began, a twinkle in his eyes.

'Oh, please stop,' Paige interrupted. 'You're ruining a perfectly lovely flower!'

He raised his eyebrows at her. 'Oh? But in the process I might find out what I really want to know.'

She flushed. 'Don't be ridiculous, Chad. You know how I feel about our relationship. So don't try to make jokes.'

'I think there's been a mistake. I certainly don't know how you feel about our relationship. I know how you feel about relationships in general—this "communion of the spirit", which obviously you don't feel with the handsome Stephen McCall either—but our relationship is a mystery to me. I don't know what to make of it at all.'

Paige ventured a glance at Chad, only to see that he appeared to be quite serious. There was a line between his eyebrows, and his amber eyes had a depth that she had never seen there before. She looked away quickly, knowing how his eyes had affected her at other times. Maybe she had been foolish to agree to come along with him today.

'I—I think we'd better be going,' she said, starting to get up.

But Chad reached out an arm and gently pulled her back to her seat on the rock. 'No, don't do that,' he said softly. 'You talk about feeling something special for the man you love. But it seems to me that you're always running, not only from me, but from Stephen McCall.' He placed a finger over her lips when she would have objected vehemently. 'Oh, yes, Paige Brownell, you *are* running from him, or you wouldn't be here with me now. How can you ever learn to feel anything for anyone if you're always running away?'

It was a good question, a heartfelt one, if the intensity behind Chad's expression was genuine.

'I don't run away,' she began, then she stopped. She *did* run away, had run away from Stephen because she didn't feel any physical attraction, had been running away from Chad Smith because she felt too much. It was a paradox which she was at a loss to explain. Fitfully, she rose before he could stop her and walked along the path for a short distance, leaving Chad sitting alone on the rock.

A weeping willow, its branches sweeping low over the bank, was ahead of her, and just where the branches brushed the path a log had fallen and blocked her way. She dodged under the willow, unaware that Chad had risen from his seat to follow her.

He caught up with her beneath the curtaining branches of the willow tree. She turned to face him through the wavering light and shadow, unsure of herself and, most of all, unsure of him. She didn't know whether she would read anger in his face, or lust, or annoyance. She was totally unprepared for what she found.

In the soft pale green half-light beneath the sheltering branches of the willow tree with the green fresh fragrant scent of the tree wafted around them by the gentle breeze across the marsh, she stared up at him. His amber eyes rested upon her mouth for a brief moment before moving to her eyes. And the message on his face was not anger or annoyance or even lust. It was perplexity, bewilderment, confusion. Not what she had expected from Chad, who was always so sure of himself, who was experienced with women.

She couldn't have stopped herself even if she had wanted to. She reached out to him as he reached for her, and as his strong arms went around her, she closed her eyes and pressed her face to his chest. Then he was kissing her, but not with the stirring passionate kisses to which she had grown accustomed. These were tender kisses that he rained upon her forehead, her lips, her throat, and in the open neckline of her shirt.

The unexpected gentleness did not restrain the force of desire that always swept over her when she was in Chad's arms. She clung to him, wondering if she was losing her mind. That was, if she still had a mind to lose. It seemed as though any free will she might have had was evaporating, as though her determination to avoid him had swirled away, as though her distrust of Chad's motives had been only a trick of her imagination.

Gently he pulled away, disengaged his lips from hers, removed his hands and let them hang at his sides. They stared at each other for a long moment. Paige's lips were slightly parted and she could feel her pulse pounding, pounding against her temples. Around them the willow branches swayed, light rippled and wove itself through the leaves. The light's motion made her feel as though she was unsteady on her feet.

'We'd better go back,' Chad said finally, and without another word he turned quickly, parted the willow branches, and walked purposefully back to where the horses waited, leaving Paige to follow behind as she tried to sort through the tangle of her jumbled emotions.

CHAPTER EIGHT

SHE had seen Chad in many moods, Paige reflected later when she was walking briskly along the path to the Manse, but she wasn't any closer to determining which was the real Chad Smith than she had been when she first arrived on St Albans. Passionate, friendly, annoyed, perplexed, witty—never had she known a man with so many sides. Dealing with him left her feeling completely at a loss; she never knew which facet would present itself. Just when she had become convinced that she had learned to handle one side of his personality, he would turn into an entirely different person.

Today, for example. His funny bumpkin act in front of Stephen showed his delight in tricking someone into thinking he was something other than what he was. The way he had acted on the dock after lunch had been altogether pleasant and likeable. And on the bridle trail when they had stopped to rest, he had seemed sincere about exploring her feelings about their relationship. Later, under the weeping willow, she had seen a different Chad, a Chad who had seemed just as bewildered as she. But which was the real Chad? And what exactly did she feel for him?

One good thing about their outing to the stable —she had learned how to run the ChrisCraft. Chad hadn't noticed how carefully she watched him, and now she felt confident enough to take the boat out alone.

But first there was the problem of Stephen McCall.

Much to Paige's relief, Chad had swung off along the forest route to the Sea House as soon as they had secured *Paige One* at her mooring. In the half-light of approaching dusk, she entered the Manse by the back

133

door and found Stephen sitting at the kitchen table drinking a beer and eating a ham-and-cheese sandwich.

She flipped on the overhead light. 'I see you've made yourself at home,' she commented.

'I didn't expect you to cook my dinner for me,' he said. 'It'd be that way if we lived together, too. I'm so used to fending for myself that you wouldn't have to feel as though you were taking on new responsibilities, and——'

'Stephen, please. I'm not going to share an apartment with you, and that's that.' She found the ham and the cheese in the refrigerator and began slapping a sandwich together for herself.

'Did you have fun on your boat ride?' asked Stephen, deciding to try a new tack.

'Um-hmm,' she said noncommittally.

'This handyman of yours——'

'Of my aunts',' she reminded him.

'Are you in love with him?' Stephen's tone was sharp; he had meant to startle her with the question, and he had succeeded.

'I—of course not. He's the handyman here, for heaven's sake.' But her hands trembled as she set the top piece of bread on her sandwich.

'I caught a glimpse of him when he was on the way to the boat dock. He gives quite a different impression when he's cleaned up a bit.'

'Chad is—a man of many moods,' Paige said tersely.

Stephen watched her appraisingly as she sat down across from him. At this point she wished she had never made the sandwich. Her mouth had gone dry, and she had completely lost her appetite. In love with Chad Smith? She had never dared to ask herself that question, but now that Stephen had asked it, there was no way to avoid it. Yet the present situation hardly afforded her a chance to think about it.

Somehow, with Stephen watching her wordlessly from across the table, she managed to choke down her sandwich. Afterwards, when she had washed the dishes, he said, 'How about a walk on the beach? It's a pleasant night, and I think we need the time together.'

Paige was totally unwilling to put herself in a situation that might lead to Stephen's getting the wrong idea. She shook her head. 'We *don't* need time together.'

'I suppose you're right. You have something important to think about.' Stephen's confident smile was beginning to look worn around the edges.

Paige studied his face for any sign that he realised what was really on her mind, and decided that he did not. 'Yes, I do have things to think about,' she said quietly, knowing that the important thing she would be thinking about would not be Stephen McCall.

She knew that, for her own sake, she had to get away from him immediately. 'I'll make up the bed in the guest room for you while you're walking on the beach,' she said hurriedly over her shoulder as she left him standing alone in the kitchen and looking after her with an expression of unremitting disappointment on his face.

After she had prepared the guest room, she went to the peaceful haven of her own room, where she lay in her bed, staring up at the ceiling.

Was she in love with Chad Smith? No, she thought, trying to convince herself. She couldn't be in love with him, not until she had investigated him to her satisfaction. Tomorrow, she thought, tomorrow after Stephen had left, she would take *Paige One* into Brunswick and try to find someone who knew Chad. She was beginning to hope desperately that whatever she found out about Chad Smith would exonerate him of any trace of wrongdoing.

It was over an hour before she heard Stephen's purposeful tread on the stairs, and she caught her breath as she heard his footsteps stop outside her door and a hand touch her doorknob. But if he had been planning to come in, he apparently thought better of it, because he walked on, and she heard the click of the latch as he went into the guest room and closed the door.

She slept late in the morning, not even hearing Stephen as he showered in the bathroom next to her room. Nor did she awaken when he went downstairs and prepared his own breakfast. It was not until he gently pushed her bedroom door open that she finally opened her eyes and focused blearily on Stephen's handsome face as he leaned over her bed, one hand resting on either side of her pillow.

'Good morning,' he said.

'Stephen! You should have knocked before you came into my room!' She pulled the bedclothes up over her chest and struggled to a sitting position.

'I was afraid you'd tell me to go away. Would you have?' His brilliant blue eyes rested on hers, and in them she read unabashed longing.

'I would have asked you to wait a minute and I would have dressed, and then I would have come out to tell you that——'

'That you'll come back to New York with me?'

'That I haven't changed my mind. You're going back to New York alone.' Paige spoke as firmly as she could in the circumstances, still feeling slightly muzzy from sleep.

Stephen's expression became bleak. 'There's no chance? If you think about it for a while longer?'

Paige shook her head emphatically. 'No chance, Stephen.' Her voice softened at his crestfallen look, although she knew that there was no meaningful way to soften the blow. 'I—I'm sorry I can't go along with it.'

Stephen straightened. 'I'm sorry, too, Paige,' he said stiffly. He might have said more, but just as he was about to speak, they both heard Chad's unmistakable whistling as he clattered up the stairs.

Chad saw Stephen through the open door of her

room. And in the bed on the other side of Stephen he saw Paige, who despite her innocence couldn't help but flush with embarrassment.

The colour seemed to drain from Chad's face, but he recovered enough to flash Paige a look of pure resentment. Their eyes locked for only a moment, but it was long enough for Paige to see in them the condemnation and contempt he felt for her.

'Chad,' she whispered in spite of herself, slowly shaking her head to and fro. It was a plea for understanding and a cry of anguish, all wrapped up in the single syllable of his name.

She didn't know whether he heard her or not, because he turned angrily and fled down the stairs, as though the sight of her occupying the same bedroom with Stephen was more than he could stomach.

'So that's it,' mused Stephen, searching her face. 'There is something between you two, after all. I might have guessed!'

'No! That's not it. There isn't anything between us at all,' and the pain in her voice communicated itself to Stephen.

He studied her carefully for a moment. 'Any fool can see that if there's nothing between you now, there soon will be if you continue to live on this godforsaken island together. And believe me,' he went on, regaining some of his old assurance, 'I have no desire to sit around and watch it happen.' His eyes grew hard; he seemed resigned.

'Goodbye, Stephen.'

'Goodbye, Paige.' He wheeled abruptly and was gone.

When the sound of the helicopter had faded over the marsh in the direction of Brunswick, Paige pulled a housecoat on over her short gown and went in search of Chad. She felt a compulsion to explain, to be understood. She couldn't let Chad go on thinking what he so obviously believed, that she and Stephen had

spent the night in bed together. She had convinced
Chad that her scruples wouldn't allow her to go to bed
with a man she didn't love, and she became almost
frantic when she thought that Chad might believe that
she loved Stephen. And worse yet, what if he thought
she didn't love Stephen? What if Chad thought that she
actually had gone to bed with a man she didn't love?

She found him, finally, by following the sound of the
axe. He was chopping wood at the edge of the forest,
working in a frenzy, the axe glinting in the sunlight,
chips of wood flying. Her heart gave a little leap when
she first saw him. He was bare to the waist, and his
muscles, slick with sweat, rippled as he repeatedly raised
the axe high over his head and brought it down to split
the logs into firewood.

He didn't appear to hear her when she first spoke his
name, so she cleared her throat and spoke louder the
second time. He turned and stared at her, panting with
exertion, his expression angry.

'I came to explain,' she began, but he cut her off
short.

'You aren't required to explain anything to me,' he
said curtly, hefting the axe again.

'Wait,' she said unhappily. 'It wasn't the way you
think. Stephen hoped to catch me off guard by
surprising me in my room. He slept in the guest room
all night. You must believe me!'

Chad took in her embarrassment, her distraught appearance, her simple housecoat. 'He's gone, I see, off into the wild blue yonder,' he said with a hint of sarcasm.

'He—he wanted me to go back with him, but I
wouldn't go.'

'So it's over between you?' Chad's question was
sharply asked.

Paige nodded. 'It never even really began,' she said.

Chad heaved a sigh and leaned on his axe handle.
'Your spirits never managed to commune?' He seemed
to be repressing a smile.

'Please don't laugh at me,' she said imploringly. She twisted nervously at a loose button on the front of her housecoat.

Chad sobered instantly, studying every inch of her face, weighing her obvious distress. Under his scrutiny, she shrank, knowing that despite her denials, he was probably thinking the worst.

She was completely surprised that when he spoke, it was with sincerity and more kindness than she could have imagined. 'I'm not laughing at you, Paige. In fact, I think you handled Mr McCall very well. And I don't believe anything happened between you last night, although I must admit it was quite a shock when I saw him in your bedroom. My thoughts certainly ran the gamut!' He shook his head. 'Next time you entertain a man in your bedroom, how about warning me in advance?'

His tone was light, and his eyes were warm. Paige felt a rush of relief. 'Oh, Chad,' she said, 'you know I'm not going to be entertaining any man in my bedroom.' She smiled at him, and for an instant there was a flash of communication between them. It was the kind of communication that often passes between two good friends, the kind of friends who don't have to talk to understand what the other is feeling. But then, remembering her plans for the day, she became suddenly serious and knew she had to retreat.

'I—I'll leave you to your work,' she stammered, effectively ending the meaningful moment before turning and almost running back to the Manse.

After Chad's wholehearted expression of faith in her, she felt like a traitor. There was no way she could reciprocate his faith as long as he persisted in remaining a man of mystery. Today she was going to spend her day checking up on him as planned, because for her own peace of mind, checking up on him was what she had to do, if only for the aunts' sake. And she was determined that she wouldn't let his charm—or his faith in her—divert her from the task. She only wished she didn't feel like such a sneak about it.

She dressed in white slacks and a navy-blue blazer with gold buttons; around her hair, to protect it from the wind and salt spray, she wound a red, white and blue silk scarf. After a quick breakfast, she looked around the Manse to make sure that Chad had not reappeared; then she hurried to the dock and uncovered the new boat. She wanted to get away before he found out she was going.

It was easier than she had expected. The big inboard motor started smoothly, and she eased the ChrisCraft away from the dock without problems. She would be well on her way to Brunswick before Chad even realised that she was gone.

The weather was cooler this morning, and Paige was glad she had worn her long-sleeved blazer. The wind whipped back around the windshield, flapping the edges of her jacket in the wind. She buttoned the blazer, then turned her attention back to the boat. It was an easy-handling craft, she found much to her relief.

She landed the boat at the picturesque shrimp docks on Bay Street in downtown Brunswick. The shrimp fleet had left the dock earlier; the only shrimp boats there were those that for one reason or another weren't going out. Here the air smelled of an odd mixture of brine and machine oil. There were a few onlookers, mostly tourists, and one taciturn fellow with a red beard and an upstanding thatch of red hair who helped her tie up her boat without saying a word.

'I have business to attend to in town,' she told him, and he nodded.

'Figured you did. Don't worry, I'll keep an eye on your boat.' He ran an appraising eye over the ChrisCraft. 'Looks like the one Chad Smith was going to buy. Is it?'

'Yes, it is,' she replied, thinking rapidly. Perhaps this man knew Chad and could tell her something about him. 'Are you a friend of Chad's?' she asked brightly in a conversational tone.

'Nope,' he said. 'But I know him, all right.'

Paige couldn't figure out from his expression whether his opinion of Chad was good or bad.

'Have you known him long?'

The man fixed her with a long thoughtful look. 'I guess I've known him long enough to know that he wouldn't want me talking about his business,' and with that he walked away and leaned against a tar-spattered piling, folded his arms across his chest, and stared out across the water.

Chastened, Paige left the dock and walked up the street. Still, it was encouraging to find someone who knew Chad. It meant that there might be others, others who would not be as reluctant to tell her what they knew about him.

Brunswick was much as she remembered it—small town, but well kept. She passed a new county library, and noticed that several storefronts had been painted or remodelled. She stopped at the post office to pick up the mail. There was a letter in Aunt Biz's handwriting; she stuffed it in her bag to read later. She was in a hurry to get to the bank.

The aunts' bank hadn't changed much, so she was unprepared when she went inside and saw that the personnel all seemed different from the ones she remembered. There had been a railing here, she thought as she stood in front of the bank president's office, and the tellers had worked in cages instead of behind those bright Formica counters. She was roused from her reverie when a cool voice said, 'Yes, may I help you?'

She swivelled around to face Glynis McGuire.

She was totally unprepared to encounter Glynis's pointed cat face and turquoise eyes here, and she was so surprised that she momentarily forgot what she had been planning to say. At least, she noted with satisfaction, Glynis seemed equally surprised to see her.

They stood and stared blankly at each other for a moment.

To her credit, Paige recovered first. 'Hello, Glynis,' she managed to say. 'I've come to see the president of the bank. It used to be Mr Lingfelt,' and she craned her head around to look in the office beyond, wondering if it was still Mr Lingfelt.

'It's Mr Hightower now,' Glynis told Paige. Her voice was businesslike, brusque. 'I don't know if he has time to see you or not.' Glynis made a show of leafing through several pages of the appointment book that occupied a prominent spot on her desk. There was a typewriter, file folders—Paige surmised that Glynis was Hightower's secretary. And guardian dragon, from the look of her.

Glynis looked up from the book and narrowed her eyes at Paige. 'Would you mind telling me what you want to see him about?'

'It's a private matter,' she said, hoping this would discourage Glynis.

'I'll see if I can squeeze you in,' Glynis said finally, slapping the book closed and mincing on too-high heels across the plush carpet to Mr Hightower's door. A whispered conference, a cough, a high-voiced remonstrance. Then at last Glynis returned. 'He'll see you now,' she told Paige.

Paige paused at the door of the office, sizing up the man she had come to see. Instead of Mr Lingfelt's comfortable pear shape, this man was spare and lean. Instead of Mr Lingfelt's shiny bald head, a sparse slick covering of greasy black hair. And instead of Mr Lingfelt's round friendly face, a hawk-nosed, sharp-chinned expression of annoyance.

'Yes, what can I do for you?' Jacob Hightower was decidedly impatient.

'I'm Paige Brownell,' she said, stepping forward and extending her hand. His handshake was cold and limp. 'My aunts are Sophie and Biz Farrier. I believe you handle their financial affairs.'

Hightower nodded. 'Yes. I don't see how that concerns you.'

Paige refused to be intimidated. 'It concerns me very much,' she said briskly. 'I'm worried about my aunts' financial situation, and I thought that maybe you could answer a few questions for me.'

'I don't want to violate my clients' privacy,' said Hightower, his thin lips set in a prim line.

'I understand that. But I am their family, the only real family they have, and your bank has been in charge of the Farrier family trust for many years now. And I'd like to know what part Chad Smith plays in my aunts' financial affairs.'

Hightower fixed his protruding eyes on her for a long moment before leaning forward over his desk.

'I'm not prepared to tell you actual dollars and cents. That's what I thought you wanted to know, the extent of their fortune. But I don't mind saying that your aunts have given Chad Smith their power of attorney. So he plays quite an important part in their financial dealings.'

Paige had been sitting on the edge of her chair, but she was so stunned at this startling information that she leaned back and stared at Jacob Hightower. Never in her wildest imaginings had she dreamed that Aunt Sophie and Aunt Biz would take such drastic action.

She knew that power of attorney meant that Chad had been appointed to act for the aunts in legal and finanical matters, and that usually power of attorney was conferred by those who are ill and unable to conduct their own affairs. In effect, in the aunts' case, this meant that Chad Smith exercised complete control over their money. Aunt Biz and Aunt Sophie were in good health; why would they turn everything over to Chad? Unless, and the thought made her feel sick, Chad had coerced them.

'Just—just what does Chad do?' she queried.

'He decides where their money should be spent,

directs their investments, handles transactions. I suggest that, if you want to know more about it, you ask him.'

Paige drew a deep breath and rose abruptly from her seat. 'I will,' she said darkly. 'You can be sure of that.' A brief goodbye, and then she was facing Glynis, who had been standing much too close to the door.

'Tell Chad that I have those papers ready for him,' said Glynis with a knowing smile. 'I'm sure he'll be eager to see them.' Paige stared blankly at Glynis for a moment, then brushed past her, trying her best to remain calm. Tell Chad, indeed? She'd have something to tell Chad, that was for sure.

Afterwards, she could barely recall her boat journey back to St Albans. Her mind was reeling with unsettling thoughts; she simply could not fathom how the aunts could turn control of their money over to an itinerant handyman! Why, it was madness! And the question she had been asking herself over and over since Stephen had first asked it seemed equal madness. How could she have ever thought she was in love with Chad Smith?

She tied the ChrisCraft at the dock and ran up the path to the Manse. No sign of Chad here; she tried to think of where he might be working. He wasn't in the basement either, and a glance towards the edge of the forest showed a neatly stacked pile of firewood, but Chad was gone. Paige attempted to calm herself; she didn't want to look like a crazy woman when she confronted him. She took time to hurry upstairs and discard her navy-blue blazer, too hot for this time of day. She took off the scarf and smoothed her hair. Her reflection stared back at her, a picture of a young woman who was clearly distraught. She put her hands over her face for a moment, willing herself to relax. She wanted to be composed and in charge of herself when she presented Chad with what she knew.

Downstairs, she stood on the front porch, wondering where to look first. The Sea House, perhaps, or should she check the lean-to where the Mule was stored? No point in looking for Chad if he had taken the golf cart and gone on an excursion to some remote part of the island.

The problem of his whereabouts was solved when she heard singing, full-bodied robust singing, coming from the direction of Aunt Biz's garden patch. So that was where he was! Paige hurried around the corner of the house and along the path through the woods. She came to the clearing where Aunt Biz always planted her garden—and stopped in consternation.

It was Chad, all right, hoeing between the rows. She couldn't figure out what tune it was that he was singing; he stopped when he saw her.

'So you're back from your little jaunt in the new boat,' he said amiably, not seeming to mind that she had gone out alone. 'If I'd known you were here, I wouldn't have been singing that song. It's not fit for a lady's ears, I'm afraid. Hope it didn't offend you.'

Paige hadn't been paying any attention to the words, but he had effectively deflected her from what she had been planning to say. 'I'm not offended,' she said. 'I didn't really hear it.'

'Good. It's an old sea shanty, English, I think.' Chad presented a peculiar picture, leaning on Aunt Biz's hoe as he was. It was a pose that was definitely out of character for him. 'I thought I'd better hoe the garden,' he explained. 'I can't imagine why, but Aunt Biz does this once a week or so. I haven't tried it before, and don't care to try it again. I've never figured out what the purpose of hoeing is, have you?'

'Weeds,' said Paige distractedly. 'It's supposed to get rid of the weeds.' How could she confront Chad when he ran his eyes over her so disarmingly, how could she accuse when she melted at the very sight of him? She gathered herself together; she looked him straight in the eye. She made herself plunge ahead.

'Chad, I've been to my aunts' bank,' she said bluntly. There was no point in beating around the bush.

Chad stared at her incredulously. He raised his eyebrows and waited for her to go on.

'I talked with Mr Hightower. He told me——' In mid-sentence she was losing her nerve. She swallowed; her throat was unaccountably dry.

'He told you what?' Chad's voice was neutral; it didn't give anything away.

'He told me that you control my aunts' money. I want to know why.' She stood watching him, unaware that she was breathing faster than normal. A bee buzzed around her head, landed on her hair. Chad, within arm's reach, put out a hand to brush it away. She thought he had other intentions; she was unaware of the bee. She flinched, stepped backward; her face seemed unnaturally white in the bright sunlight. Too late she saw the bee buzzing away in search of a more accommodating flower, and realised that Chad had only been protecting her. Embarrassed at her skittishness, she turned away.

Chad sighed and threw down the hoe. 'Well, that's enough hoeing for one day. I wasn't cut out to be a gardener, anyway.' He stood there, rubbing the back of his neck, as though trying to decide what to do next.

'I don't think you were cut out to be a handyman, either,' said Paige, unable to resist saying it. She lifted her head and saw that he was regarding her in a manner that could only be described as rueful. As though he wanted to say something, but couldn't. Or wouldn't. Or perhaps shouldn't.

'Maybe you're right,' he replied, appearing to think this over. Silence for a moment, then he said, 'Look, Paige, can we talk this over? Or are you now so convinced that I'm a cad and a fortune-hunter that there's no point in it? Can you listen to reason?'

Paige considered this. She wanted things explained, wanted all the pieces to fit neatly and happily together. Most of all, she wanted to know that Aunt Biz and Aunt Sophie were safe, not victims of their own kindness to a stray. She sighed. 'All right. Let's go somewhere and you can tell me your side of the story. That is, if you will.'

Chad didn't say anything, but he took her hand and led her through the rows of cabbages, tomato vines, and pepper plants. Aunt Biz had placed a wooden park bench beneath a persimmon tree at the edge of the clearing. They sat on it and Chad half-turned to face her.

'I don't really know how to begin explaining this,' he told her. 'Why don't you just tell me what you know?'

'I know only what I've told you—that you have control of my aunts' money, money that's been in my family for generations. Aunt Biz always took such pride in her management of the trust. I can't understand her giving it up. Especially to you.'

Chad looked off into the distance. When he looked back at her, he seemed sincere enough. He shrugged with a little smile. 'She wanted to. That's all I can tell you.'

'She *wanted* to turn control of her money over to a complete stranger?'

'I'm not exactly a complete stranger. I've lived here for months, and I treat the aunts like my own. I like them, and they trust me. That's all there is to it.' Chad met her sceptical gaze steadily.

'That's not all there is to it, Chad Smith!' Paige was growing angry that he would think her so gullible. 'What did you say or do to make them "trust you?" '

'I didn't have to do or say anything. And I might add that your aunts' money has never been safer.'

'Safe? You can go out and buy an expensive new boat without their permission and I'm supposed to believe that their money is safe?'

'Calm down, calm down,' said Chad, placing a restraining hand on her arm. 'You agree that they need the boat. There's no harm in it. They'll be delighted when they see it.'

'Yes, but don't you understand? How do they know that you're not spending money right and left? How do *I* know that you're not stashing it away someplace for the day you just up and decide to leave here, how do I know that you're not squandering it on useless playthings or——'

She stopped talking; she had a staggering thought. Those horses in the stable, the beautiful horses so obviously of good breeding. The deference of the stable attendant, a respect not usually accorded to a wandering handyman who was allowed to exercise the horses in his spare time. Max and Damien—had they perhaps been bought with her aunts' money?

All at once Paige was certain that the horses belonged to Chad. She should have known it when she saw him with them and noticed the way they both responded to him. And where else would someone like Chad get the money to buy thoroughbreds of such high quality?

'Paige, I'm not squandering your aunts' money. I give you my word. And I have no need of useless playthings. I——' but he stopped and seemed unwilling to finish the sentence. 'You'll just have to take my word for it, I guess,' he said grimly.

'Take your word for it? How can I take your word for anything? I don't even know you. Your background, your reason for being here—I know nothing about you!' Her voice had risen uncontrollably; her hands were clenched in her lap.

'You know a few things about me,' Chad said smoothly. 'We know each other rather well, you and I. This morning, when you begged me to believe that there was nothing between you and Stephen despite rather incriminating circumstances, I knew you well enough to know you were speaking the truth. Trust me, Paige.'

He put a finger beneath her chin, tilted her head upward so that she had to look at him. The expression on his face was intense and earnest; she sensed a wavering in his position, a tentative lowering of the façade, almost as though he willed her to guess his secret.

For a moment, a split second, she nearly thought that he might be willing to stop whatever game he was playing and reveal himself to her. But no, it was not to be. He had closed himself away from her. She wrenched herself out of reach, thinking she wanted to get as far away from him as possible.

But he wouldn't let her go. When she would have stood up and run back through the garden and along the path to the Manse, he grabbed her by the shoulders and with surprising force held her where she was. She bent her head, weakened by his show of strength. She was no match for him, and she knew it.

'Look at me,' he said, and his voice was surprisingly gentle. Slowly she raised her face to his. He was staring down at her, his expression unfathomable.

He spoke, and his words were measured and carefully spoken. 'Paige, I wouldn't lie to you. I'm doing your aunts no harm, I swear it. Believe me.'

How could she not believe him when he spoke so convincingly? He had shown his concern for her aunts in countless ways; why would she think that he would treat them unscrupulously? Her instinct told her to trust him, and yet her common sense wouldn't let her.

'I—I'm going to talk to Aunt Sophie and Aunt Biz about your handling of their money,' she said haltingly. 'I'm going to find out what you did to convince them that you should be in charge of it.'

Chad's gaze didn't waver. 'Go ahead,' he said, daring her. His hands still grasped her shoulders, and she arched backwards to put distance between them.

Then it was happening again—she was whirled away in a vortex of passion in spite of herself. He lowered his head slowly, slowly, so slowly that her mind had time to register the birdsong overhead and the whispering of the leaves in the breeze. It couldn't be happening again, but it was, and in an agony of pleasure she thought, *only for a moment*, and then lost herself in anguished expectancy. Chad's lips took hers softly, then with breathtaking intimacy. And, as always, she responded, forgetting her doubts, her uncertainties, and all her fears. For a moment there was only Chad, and they were together. She knew then, with agonising certainty, that she was hopelessly in love with him.

She made herself pull away from him, made herself leave the circle of his arms, made herself stand up and back away. She almost spoke, but no words seemed adequate. She wheeled and ran before he could say or do anything more.

It wasn't until much later, when she was lying in her bed that night thinking about Chad, that she remembered the letter from her aunts. She switched on the light and rummaged in her handbag. Quickly she scanned the two-page letter; it was with a sense of relief that she folded it and put it away. Aunt Sophie and Aunt Biz would be back two weeks from today.

Later, after she had turned out the light, she remembered that she had forgotten to give Chad Glynis's message.

CHAPTER NINE

IN the aftermath of her realisation that she loved Chad, one thing seemed clear. Her love for him would have to remain secondary to her aunts' best interests. Nothing would be worse than for Chad to find out how she felt about him, particularly if his intentions on St Albans were less than honourable. No matter how difficult it might be, she would have to distance herself from him both emotionally and physically, now more than ever.

In view of that condition, she thought to herself the next morning, she absolutely would not seek out Chad to tell him that Glynis had papers ready for him. Anyway, what kind of papers were they? Something to do with his management of her aunts' money, no doubt. Well, she had no intention of acting as a go-between in this business. She would have to talk with Aunt Biz and Aunt Sophie first and find out why they had been seemingly rash enough to assign him their power of attorney.

Chad would be working in the dining room this morning; he had painted two walls, and would finish the job today. She looked around the big kitchen with satisfaction. It was much more cheerful now that the walls were bright canary yellow, and she herself had washed, starched, ironed and hung the limp eyelet-ruffled curtains at the windows. The dining-room walls were now a subdued ivory, and when the red velvet curtains had been shaken free of dust and rehung, the room would shine with its former elegance.

Speaking of Chad, he would be arriving soon to paint. She planned to clear out, so that they wouldn't have to meet. She dreaded seeing him again, was afraid that somehow he, who could read her only too well, would sense her love for him. It seemed like a perfect time to take the Mule and ride to the north end of St Albans to explore the now defunct fishermen's village and look for those old tabby ruins of the early settlers' cabins.

A detour to her room to get her sketchbook, and a hasty pass through the kitchen to collect enough miscellaneous items for lunch. Bread, ham, cheese, and a jar of homemade dill pickles. And a few cans of cola, wrapped in layers of newspaper so they would stay cold. A basket to put it all in, and then down the path to the lean-to which housed the Mule.

The golf cart was a splendid way to get about on the island, Paige thought as it hummed along the path. It was quiet and didn't disturb the wildlife. She was hoping she would spot a deer today as she drove deeper into the woods. As a child she had often surprised deer feeding near the path, surprisingly tame animals that usually looked up with a mildly startled expression before going back to their grazing. Hunting had never been allowed on the island, and they knew they had nothing to fear from man.

The path widened into a sandy road that led between two rows of cabins that had served as homes for the fishermen. Trees, massive willow oaks, sheltered the road from the sun. The deserted air of the little village seemed an odd contrast to the picture of the place in Paige's memory; the cabins had always overflowed with lively, cheerful people, people who didn't have much but were always willing to share what they had. She pulled the Mule up beside a chinquapin tree in one of the front yards and got out to look around.

Glass had been blown out of some of the windows, and here and there a door swung lopsided on a hinge. Weeds sprouted around front steps, fallen leaves settled in heaps in the corners of porches. The deserted look of the place might have been depressing if the village were not so picturesque.

Paige returned to the Mule to get her sketching materials, then looked around her with an artist's eyes. Perhaps she could draw that dilapidated cabin with the morning glory trailing along the porch rail. Or that old dinghy, rotting now, on the sunny side of the biggest cabin, where a scarlet locust's showy flowers drooped beguilingly over the gunwales. She squinted her eyes at the scarlet locust and tried to imagine how it would look worked in a needlepoint design.

She sat down in front of one of the willow oaks and began to draw. It was a challenge to shade the dinghy just so, making the golden sunlight as much a part of the picture as the cabin was, or the dinghy, or the scarlet locust. Her task absorbed her, and she paused only briefly to wolf down a sandwich. When she had finally finished her meticulously detailed drawing, she stood and stretched. To her surprise, the sun had sunk low in the sky. It was much later than she had thought it was, and she still hadn't looked for those old tabby ruins.

Perhaps she had time after all, she thought, with a dubious glance upward. The sky was darkening much faster now, and she could hear the sound of breakers on the ocean side of the island, meaning that the sea was rougher than usual. Well, she'd drive the Mule down the side path where she thought the ruins were, and if she didn't see any trace of them, she'd come back another day.

The foxtail grass beside the path was bending in the wind; Paige steered the Mule carefully, but not at top speed. If she drove too fast, she might miss the ruins she was looking for. She stopped when she saw a pile of grey in the middle of a clearing, but it turned out to be only a heap of oyster shells, placed there once for some long-forgotten reason. Before she started up the Mule again, she thought she heard someone calling her name. She listened, but all she heard was the rattle of palmetto fronds in the wind.

Further on there was a bend in the path, and as she rounded it, she saw what she was looking for straight ahead. A low wall, crumbling on top, and almost covered by Virginia creeper vines. She stopped the Mule, got out, picked her way carefully through the weeds to the wall. Yes, this was it—the walls made a square, and there was an opening where the door must have been, and steps leading to the inside of what had once been a structure. Not far away she saw another such ruin, and excitedly she made her way to it.

This had been a bigger building, very large, perhaps some sort of public house. She ran her hand along the top of the wall. Oyster shells protruded from the strong cement-like bonding material. The tabby had withstood the years well.

The large building was not as grown over with vines. Paige stepped over the wall where it was no more than a foot high and nudged an oyster shell with her sandalled foot. Her foot struck something solid; she found a sturdy stick and dug at it.

She pried loose from the earth some sort of pottery, a bowl. It was cracked and a big piece was missing from the edge, but it was a bowl nonetheless. This might have belonged to the first settlers in this area, people who had lived on St Albans perhaps two hundred and fifty years ago. She would take it back to the Manse; maybe the aunts would know who had lived here before her own ancestors arrived.

She barely noticed how her hair was beginning to blow in the wind that was whipping inland from the ocean side of the island. A carved design on a piece of pottery had claimed her attention, and she dug at the dirt that was caked in the grooves with a fingernail. This time she didn't step over the wall as she had before; instead she decided to climb over the old stairs. She didn't see the rattlesnake or hear the ominous buzz of its rattles until it was too late. The snake, a small ground rattler, lashed at her sandalled foot, lightning swift.

At first she only felt surprise and a detached feeling that it couldn't be happening. Then the pain struck, and she heard herself scream. The bowl slipped out of her hands, shattering into several pieces.

She would have fallen, but strong arms encircled her and supported her. She would have fainted and welcomed the oblivion, but such was her amazement that someone was there to help her that she fought to maintain consciousness.

'I'll carry you,' said Chad, assessing the situation immediately and taking in the two fang marks on her big toe.

'The snake,' she said, gritting her teeth against the intense pain that was shooting up her leg. She remembered about snakes from Uncle John's lectures on the subject years ago when her aunts and her mother worried about her roaming the island. She knew that the snake should be killed or captured in order to determine what treatment was necessary for the bite. Different species of snakes, different treatment.

'Gone,' said Chad. He looked around, still supporting her in his strong arms. 'You didn't see what kind it was, did you?'

'A ground rattler,' she gasped. 'I'm positive.'

He swung her up, strode through the undergrowth, set her down on the Mule's seat. By this time tears of pain were rolling down her cheeks. Chad slid his belt off and fastened it around the calf of her leg in a makeshift tourniquet. Already her toe was swelling and beginning to discolour.

'We're going back to the Sea House,' said Chad, jumping into the Mule and starting it up. He drove fast, almost recklessly, steering the Mule around the bends of the path without heed for obstacles such as pine cones, tree roots, or loose sticks. He kept one arm around Paige's shoulders to keep her from lurching out of the Mule.

They reached the Sea House faster than Paige would have believed possible. Chad carried her inside, nudging the door open with his shoulder. He laid her carefully on the wool serape that covered his bed.

'I have a snakebite kit,' he said tersely, taking a box from a drawer.

'Do you—do you know what to do?' she asked faintly. She felt suddenly very weak and nauseated.

'Yes, of course,' he said.

'Shouldn't you get me to a hospital?' A strong, frightening sense of their isolation on St Albans swept over her.

'I should—but I can't.' Paige looked up and saw the bleakness behind his eyes. 'There's a tropical storm out to sea, and it's heading this way. It wouldn't be safe for us to take the boat out now—the seas are already so high that we'd be swamped before we got halfway to Brunswick. I'm sorry.'

Paige closed her eyes against the waves of nausea that were rolling over her, making it impossible to think. She could never have conceived of herself being in such a position, dependent on Chad Smith for her very life.

Chad knelt by the bed, his hand on her wrist. 'Your pulse rate is rising,' he said. He found a thermometer, slid it into her mouth. 'I'm going to administer the antivenin right away.'

She watched him efficiently preparing the hypodermic syringe; the pain in her leg was now so severe that she barely felt him injecting the antivenin.

He removed the thermometer from her mouth and looked at it. He did his best to hide his alarm, but she knew he was worried. Gently he washed the bite. 'I'm going to have to get the venom out,' he said. 'You know what that means, don't you?'

Numbly she nodded her head. 'Go ahead,' she murmured. The last thing she remembered was Chad removing a razor blade from the snakebite kit.

Cold, then hot. She was walking over a bed of steaming coals, she was tending a blast furnace. She was lost on a desolate Arctic tundra, until she turned her head and found herself in a desert. She tossed and cried out against the rapid images that kept flashing across her brain. A strong, cool hand, steady against her fevered brow. A damp cloth touched to her parched lips. She awoke to find Chad's face only inches from hers.

She collided with reality and remembered what had happened to her. She felt fully conscious. Chad had removed the scratchy wood serape from the bed, and she lay beneath a smooth white sheet and a lightweight thermal blanket. She saw her clothes hanging over the back of the chair beside the long table. He had undressed her, then; she stirred slightly and realised that she was nude beneath the covers. Her leg felt cold; she looked down to see that it was encased in plastic, lowered against a stool that was beside the bed.

'My clothes,' she said, surprised at how feeble her voice sounded. 'You shouldn't have——'

'I had to,' he said without a trace of apology. 'I had to sponge you with ice water to bring your temperature down. You've had a dangerously high fever.' He was matter-of-fact; she realised that now, to him, she was simply a human being who needed help. Desire and thoughts of sexual excitement had been suspended for the time being.

She closed her eyes and swallowed, gathering strength for words. But the strength wasn't there; it was an effort just to breathe.

'I've packed your leg in ice to prevent the spread of whatever venom I couldn't remove,' explained Chad, his voice hoarse. 'Paige stared up at him; there were deep dark circles beneath his eyes and his hair looked rumpled. She had vague memories of his moving through her fevered dreams, hovering anxiously over the bed. Her love for him rose in her throat, constricting it and bringing sudden tears to her eyes.

Quickly she blinked them away, hoping that he hadn't noticed.

She heard the wind outside, howling around the walls of the Sea House. Slowly she licked her lips to moisten them. 'What about the storm?' she asked when she could speak.

'It's been lashing at us now for quite a while,' Chad told her. 'I've tried to get reports on the radio, but the storm has made reception so bad that it's impossible.'

'It's not a hurricane, is it?'

'No, but a tropical storm can deliver extremely high winds.'

It was dark outside, and rain whipped at the windows. Paige could hear the crash of the waves; here on the promontory, they were exposed on three sides to water. Suddenly she was concerned for their safety in a location that was so vulnerable to the sea.

'Shouldn't we go to the Manse? We'd be safer there.'

'I don't want to move you.' Chad knelt beside her and took one of her limp hands in his stronger one. 'How do you feel?' he asked quietly.

Paige thought about it. She no longer felt nauseated, and that was perhaps a good sign. The pain was less. 'I think I feel better,' she said cautiously. 'Am I going to be all right?' Her eyes pleaded with him for reassurance.

Chad's face softened. 'You'll make it,' he said unsteadily. Then, as though he couldn't bear to talk about it, he rose quickly to his feet and went to stand in front of the fireplace, where Paige noticed for the first time that a fire had been lit. He stood with his back to her, his body silhouetted against the bright orange flames. She thought drowsily that he was really very handsome, a handsome man indeed, before she drifted off into oblivion again.

Her dream was of a tall man who stood on a high-masted sailing ship, the sea rising and falling beneath it. She had dreamed of him before, of his broad shoulders, his light hair falling across his forehead, and the face that remained in shadows until all at once he turned to her, smiled, held out his hand, and she knew it was Chad. Somehow it seemed right, this time, that she walk forward and place her hand trustingly in his. It was the trust that surprised her. She had wanted to trust him for so long.

She awoke later. It was dark outside, she still heard the wind and the breakers crashing on the beach, and at first she wasn't sure where she was. The first thing that penetrated her confusion was the fire in the fireplace. It had died to embers, but the glow was enough to softly light the small cottage. After she orientated herself, she became aware of something else—Chad's head beside hers on the pillow.

He had fallen into an exhausted sleep, punctuated by the deep breathing of one who is totally spent. He lay on his side on top of the covers, fully clothed, his head resting on one arm, his other arm lying across her stomach and his fingers lightly touching her hand. She didn't move; to do so would only wake him. And he looked as though he needed his sleep.

She turned her head slightly so that she could observe him better. His hair against the pillow looked like cloth spun of gold in the gleam of the firelight, which also touched his light brows and lashes with gilt. The circles beneath his eyes were still dark above his high rounded cheekbones. His mouth as he slept looked tender and almost vulnerable, and it bespoke a sensitivity underlying the sensuality. Watching him like this, she could almost imagine what he had looked like as a child. But he wasn't a child, she reminded herself drowsily, he was a man, a full-blooded man with a man's desires and urges. He shifted, sighed, rolled over on his back. She thought to herself that he looked like a sleeping prince.

She spent the night alternately waking and sleeping, opening her eyes occasionally to see Chad's head beside hers on the pillow and sometimes to find him checking the swelling of her foot, renewing the ice pack, or just murmuring reassuringly to her in a low voice. It was consoling, she thought sleepily, to have him near. Neither of her aunts could have been any more gentle or concerned.

Rain still curtained the windows when she awoke in the morning. Chad slept beside her in the transparent grey half-light that filled the cottage; the fire had long ago died out.

Chad opened his eyes soon after Paige opened hers. He half sat up, supporting himself on one elbow; she winced in pain as the mattress moved slightly.

'Paige?' Chad sounded concerned.

'I'm all right,' she said softly. Really, he looked so worried. His eyes were red-rimmed and anxious.

He sat up, felt her forehead, saw that she was better. His relief flitted across his face. 'Look,' he said quickly, 'I hope you don't mind my sleeping beside you last night, but I wanted to be close to you in case there was any sudden change. You were very sick.'

She nodded solemnly. 'I know,' she said. She continued to stare up at him until he leaned over and kissed her lightly on the forehead. She was all too aware of her nudity beneath the bedclothes, and she knew he was, too. He ran a finger along the side of her face, kissed her chin, and then, quickly, he stood up.

'Are you hungry?' he asked.

'A little.'

'I'll heat up a can of broth on the hot plate,' he told her, going to the cupboard and removing a can. 'It might be a good idea to stick to light food today. In any case, I don't have much food here. And with the weather as bad as it is, I don't want to go to the Manse for anything unless I have to. Besides, it probably wouldn't be a good idea to leave you alone.'

'When do you think this weather will clear up?'

Chad cast a doubtful look out of the window. 'It looks as though the storm front has stalled,' he said. 'I wish it would pass over today. You seem much better, but I still would like to take you to the hospital if possible.'

'And if we can't get to the hospital?'

'You're still going to recover. It's just that I'd like to have a doctor's official pronouncement. I have a first-aid book that tells me what to do, only I've never done it before. And I hope I never have to do it again.'

Paige hesitated before she spoke. 'You've been very kind to me,' she said haltingly.

Chad set the pan containing the broth on the hot plate and turned with one eyebrow lifted. 'Kind? Why, what else was I to do? I'd finally found you after an hour's search, and then you collapsed in my arms. I had to do something about you—how could I face Aunt Sophie and Aunt Biz if I let something happen to their favourite niece?' He was grinning at her; that must mean that he was relieved enough about her condition to make jokes.

'Their only niece,' corrected Paige.

'Right, their only niece. Therefore, also their favourite.' He turned to stir the broth.

His remark about the aunts reminded her of their letter.

'I have news from my aunts,' she told him. 'They'll be home in less than two weeks.'

'Good,' said Chad, sounding glad. He brought a cup of broth to her on a tray, and set it down on the table beside the bed.

'I'll have to sit up if I'm going to eat that,' she pointed out. 'And I don't have any clothes on.'

'I know,' said Chad speculatively.

Paige felt her face redden. 'Well, do you have a robe or something?' she asked, embarrassed.

He brought her his own bathrobe, a short one of white terrycloth, and turned his back while she slipped it on.

He found a pillow and raised her head, sliding the

pillow underneath. It lifted her only slightly. 'There,' he said. 'Do you think you can drink the broth now? I really don't think you're strong enough to sit all the way up.'

'I'll try.' She was dizzy for a moment from the change in posture. When the dizziness had passed, she sipped tentatively from the cup. The broth tasted delicious and it felt good in her empty stomach.

Chad sat in an armchair that he had pulled up beside the bed. 'Aren't you going to eat?' she asked him.

'I'll have a sandwich later, after you've gone back to sleep. I'm not really hungry.'

She finished the broth, gave him the empty cup, watched as he washed it and put it away. She was weak, but she didn't feel like sleeping. When he returned to the bed, he sat down beside her and took her hand in his. Again she felt an overwhelming sense of safety and security.

'You know,' she said after a time, 'I was lucky that you happened to be near by when the snake struck me. What were you doing down at that end of the island?'

'I was looking for you,' he explained.

'Why?'

'I could tell by the rising winds that a storm was coming up, and I knew you'd taken off in the morning. Worst of all, I knew you'd probably left the Manse to avoid me, and I would have felt responsible if you'd been caught in the storm. As a matter of fact, I even feel responsible for your having been bitten by the rattlesnake.' His eyes held a haunted look for a moment before he masked it.

'Responsible? I can't imagine why. I'd planned to explore those old ruins ever since I came to St Albans. It's not your fault that I was there at the same time the snake was.' She stared up at him, surprised that he would feel as she did.

'I made you run away because of what you think I am. And if anything had happened to you . . .' Chad

shook his head, sighed, and looked away from her
abruptly. Neither of them spoke, each too wary of the
emotion that, with any encouragement, would rise to
the surface of their relationship.

Paige dozed after a while, finally waking with a start.
Chad sat in his chair beside the bed, apparently deep in
thought. He didn't realise she was watching him until
she reached out and touched his arm gently, startling
him.

'Ah,' he said. 'You're awake. I've made some tea; I'll
pour you a cup.' He went to the cupboard and took out
a teacup.

The tea was delicious and very hot. Paige sipped at it,
noticing that Chad seemed somehow unsettled. He
paced from one end of the cottage to the other,
cracking his knuckles, fairly seething with pent-up
energy.

'Is anything wrong?' she asked when she had finished
her tea.

He shot her a probing glance. 'In a way, yes. Between
us, everything's wrong.' He walked swiftly to the bed,
leaned over her, placed one hand on the sheet on either
side of her shoulders. His eyes pierced hers. 'I've been
thinking about it while you were asleep, and I want
things to be right between us,' he said firmly but with a
hint of desperation. Paige could make no reply, only
regarded him with surprise. She had not expected such
a declaration.

He stood up straight, turned quickly and went to the
filing cabinet beside the long table. He flipped through
folders, removing several, tossing them on the table top.
She watched him, thoroughly perplexed.

He returned to her bedside and sat down beside her. It
was still grey and cloudy outside, with occasional
squalls slapping rain against the windows. He switched
on the light beside the bed so that they could more
clearly see the papers he was spreading on top of the
blanket.

Paige watched in amazement as he thrust drawing after drawing of sailboats at her. She held them in her hands, turned them over, looked at them. Chad continued to pull papers out of folders, his jaw set in a firm and determined line. 'But what is all this?' she asked when she could find her voice.

He rested his eyes on her. 'A book, Paige. I've been working on a book. That's one reason I'm at St Albans. It's a book about sailing.' His expression was authoritative and somehow serious; she didn't doubt for a moment that he was telling the truth. She felt a surge of joy and overwhelming relief that he had at last voluntarily revealed something, anything, of himself to her.

'And is this the manuscript?' She swept her eyes over the piles of papers on the bed.

'No, these are my notes, all divided into chapters. See, here's the first chapter, and here are the illustrations that go with it. Do you believe me?' His eyes nailed her; she could not look away. There was no mistaking the carefully drawn illustrations and the neat piles of papers. Chad had outlines, rough drafts, meticulously indexed notes. The evidence seemed conclusive. There was enough material here for a book, and more. She nodded.

'Good. Glynis is presently typing the final manuscript. I met her in the bank, asked her to do the typing for me in her free time. She's been working on the manuscript at home for weeks.'

'I—I thought she was a girl-friend of yours,' said Paige weakly.

'No, never. She would have liked to be, but I wasn't interested.'

'But you brought her here that night——'

'Just to help me organise some things. She might have had other things in mind, but I can assure you that I didn't, although I was tempted. I thought she might be able to get my mind off you.'

'Oh.' Paige ran her finger across the top of the blanket. There didn't seem to be much else to say.

'I came to St Albans to write this book because the island is peaceful and quiet, and I wouldn't have the interruptions I would have had anywhere else. Or the distractions. Until you came along.'

'And then I made you paint and repair things,' said Paige slowly.

'Yes. I'd always done most of my work on the book at night, though, so it wasn't too serious. Fortunately I was almost through with it.'

'My aunts knew you were writing the book?'

'No, only Glynis knew because she typed it, and I swore her to secrecy. The book had to be kept secret, Paige. I had—reasons.' He watched her to see her reaction.

Paige closed her eyes and considered this new development. It explained Glynis's message that she had papers ready for Chad. And she believed Chad when he said he was a writer; the detailed and organised papers he had shown her left no doubt in her mind that he was deeply involved in a significant writing project. The fact that Chad actually had meaningful work to do reassured her about him, and it explained the sense of purposefulness of which she had caught glimpses now and then. But the book he was writing still didn't explain why her aunts had given him control over their money.

'Now, does that make you feel better about me?' demanded Chad. Paige opened her eyes to see the stark longing in his expression, and a desire to be believed.

She felt too tired to talk any more, but she nodded her head. He hadn't explained everything yet, but it was a start. She had a definite feeling that there was more to know about Chad Smith—much more. She smiled up at him uncertainly, feeling for the first time the beginning of hope for their relationship. He must have felt it, too, because he reached across the scattered papers and grasped both her hands in his. She was aware only of a sense of deep tenderness flowing from his hands into hers as she fell into a deep and dreamless sleep.

CHAPTER TEN

DURING the following days and nights their routine settled into an intimacy that Paige would never have thought possible. The weather remained fierce; they were confined to the Sea House. The little cottage became their world. It was as if no one else existed.

After the first night, Chad prepared a pallet for himself on the floor. Paige, in the bed alone, was sometimes wakeful, and when she awoke her eyes reached for him, assuring herself that he was still there. He had become her security, and something more.

She recovered rapidly after the first day. She was able to walk by the third day, hobbling stiffly around the cottage.

'I'm sorry you were bitten by that snake,' said Chad one afternoon as he watched her standing at a window and staring out at the still-turbulent sea, 'but in a way it's helped, too. You were always running away from me before. Now you can't.' He stood behind her and slid his arms around her waist. It was a perfectly natural gesture, and she didn't stop him. They stood like that for a time, each conscious of the other's breathing. Their closeness could have easily accelerated into the enormous and powerful physicial attraction that had so often driven them in the past, but Paige was aware of a certain holding back on Chad's part and a sense of waiting on hers. It was as though each was reluctant to destroy the friendly and peaceful ambience that they had achieved. She knew that in her present weak condition, she was entirely dependent upon Chad, like it or not. And she was amazed to find that she mostly liked it.

She grew accustomed to seeing his tall figure standing

at the window or in front of the fire or at the little hot plate, heating up the endless cans of hash and soup. She found that the sound of his low voice was reassuring, that he sang in the shower. She didn't even mind his aimless whistling.

They avoided any mention at all about Chad's past. They didn't talk about money or the aunts. But their discussions ranged over so many topics that Paige couldn't keep track of them. She learned that he was knowledgeable about art, and together they looked at his drawings of sailboats, the ones that he had drawn for his book. The illustrations were extremely well done. She found out that he liked pizza, hated yogurt, and had once owned a cocker spaniel named Corky. He enjoyed the performing arts and had seen many of the same films that she had. He knew quite a bit about Europe, much to her surprise, although he didn't tell her how or when he had happened to be there. And once she was totally surprised when he began to speak to her in fluent French.

'You know, there's a lot more to you than I would have suspected,' she said to him one evening after one of their fascinating exchanges.

'How so?' he queried.

She shrugged. 'Oh, you know. You've turned out to be so knowledgeable in an eclectic way. I never would have guessed it.'

'So knowledgeable, so eclectic, when our hands touch, it's electric,' he sang, pulling her from the armchair where she sat and trying to waltz her around the room, but her foot was still sore.

'Stop!' she laughed up at him, and his eyes crinkled as he looked down at her. She thought she had never loved him more than she did at that moment while they were both happy and taking pleasure in one another's presence.

'You're right,' he said, releasing her. 'I don't want to exhaust you. And I don't want you to have a setback.

You and I have places to go and things to do, and I want you feeling fit when we do them.'

'Things to do? Like what?'

'Tomorrow the weather is going to clear. I'll take you to the doctor. And then just leave it to me. I promise you that you'll be astounded. Astonished. Amazed. And all sorts of things like that.' He grinned at her devilishly. Paige wondered what in the world he was talking about. It sounded like total nonsense to her.

'How can you tell the weather will improve?' she wanted to know.

'Old salts like me can always tell. Take my word for it. Be prepared to go to the doctor tomorrow, just like I said.'

Paige walked to the tiny mirror over the small dresser in one corner. 'I haven't washed my hair in days,' she fretted, running her fingers along one strand. 'I'll have to get clean clothes from the Manse.' Since she had been able to get out of bed, she had been alternating between the shorts and shirt she had worn the day the snake bit her and an old shirt and jeans of Chad's, both too big and too long for her.

'You'll have to move back into the Manse once the doctor says you're well,' said Chad, watching her.

She let her hand fall away from her hair and stared at his reflection in the mirror as he stood behind her. She felt all at once that she couldn't bear to let this private interlude end. During her time alone with Chad, she had grown used to the indescribably warm and gentle quality that he unfailingly displayed to her. She had grown increasingly aware of the concern and understanding that he felt for her and that she felt for him. For once, she thought, she had met a man who truly seemed to care about her in all sorts of special little ways. When she moved back into the Manse, would it all end?

Upset at the thought, she turned swiftly so that he wouldn't see in the mirror the emotion that she couldn't hide. But he blocked her way, standing behind her, and she bent her head so that he couldn't look at her face, a face that revealed all her doubts and uncertainties about their future.

Of course he knew; they had lived in such close communication that there was no way that he wouldn't pick up on her feelings now. But she couldn't bring herself to tell him that she didn't think she could bear to give up the incredibly unique bond that they had forged between them in the solitude of the Sea House.

Chad lifted her face to his, and the look that passed between them was fraught with deep meaning. She flowed into his arms, a movement so natural that it seemed that they were being moulded into one. He kissed her, and it was as it had always been between them, the passion rising up and surrounding them. He kissed her tentatively at first, but her hunger for him was so great that she opened her lips to him in eager response. As his hands began to move over her trembling body, she felt excited by the hardness of his muscles as they tensed in anticipation. She heard herself moan in aching longing, and made no objection when he lifted her in his arms and carried her to the bed.

The air around them seemed charged with electricity as Chad laid her on the rough wool serape. For a moment his eyes penetrated her, sought, found the answer he wanted. No words passed between them; words were unnecessary. He closed the gap between their lips, and all at once she felt boldly sensual, ready to yield to the strength of his passion. His mouth evoked the most overpowering sensations, his hands moved upon her body, hot and demanding.

Her hair billowed out around her head, and he slowly ran his hands up from her breasts along the sides of her neck and buried them in the dark profusion of her hair. She felt the strong hard weight of his body pressing down on hers, and she excited to the contours of him. She gasped as his lips moved slowly along her neck until they rested on the sweetly throbbing hollow at her throat.

His hands moved with agonising slowness beneath the loose shirt she wore; his seeking fingers teased her taut nipples to exquisite delight. Her soft breasts swelled beneath his gentle hands until, melting with longing, she felt that she could wait no longer.

He sensed the wanting in her and raised his head. She marvelled at his high sun-bronzed cheekbones and his light eyebrows, at the lean hard planes of his face and the utter sensuality of his mouth poised above hers. His eyes pierced her through and through, understanding her, knowing her, missing nothing.

There was no point in speaking of it; they were beyond words. It was not necessary to articulate what they both felt, an emotion that was almost visible because it was so real. They could not have put a name to it if they wanted to, but they both recognised it. It was as though they had each penetrated to the deepest reaches of the other's soul, had become a part of an extraordinary bond that was neither him nor her but a unity of both. And as they recognised this transcendence of the physical for what it was, the passion that had brought them to this juncture of their innermost beings broadened and deepened and rose into a rapturous tide of affection and tenderness that swept over them and made the physical aspects of their relationship seem unimportant.

Without speaking, Chad gathered her into his arms and held her close. Their hearts beat as one, their breathing synchronised, they closed their eyes and marvelled at it. Paige recognised it as what she had waited to experience with a man; Chad whispered her name over and over in sheer wonder at the depth of an emotion he had never dreamed existed.

They might have lain clasping each other for a minute or for an hour, they never knew how long it was. At last it was Chad who drew slightly apart. They lay on their sides, each exploring the depths of the other's eyes, touching faces, stroking hair, smiling at the sheer beauty of the two of them together.

'Chad,' she whispered, 'it's all right, you know. I—I want to be yours. Completely.'

He held her tightly, his mouth close to her ear. 'You *are* mine completely.' There was a note of fierceness underlying his gentle tone, and then he laughed softly and moved so that he could look at her face. 'At last I know what you were talking about when you confounded me with your "communion of the spirit". We can wait, darling, until your foot is officially pronounced better, until——'

Paige didn't find out what was his other reason for waiting; she didn't want to know. They only had a few more hours until dawn, until their time together in the Sea House must end. She would allow nothing to spoil it, *nothing*, she thought desperately to herself as once more she lost herself in Chad's kisses.

And when at last they feel asleep, still caught up in the unbelievability of their emotions, they remained entwined in each other's arms.

Morning brought what Chad had promised. The sun crept early through the uncurtained windows, fell across their faces and woke them. The sea had subsided into a calm and placid stretch of blue, and there was no wind, only a mild breeze that smelled of salt.

Chad smiled at her from his side of the bed, and she smiled back. He touched her lightly on the arm. 'I'll find us something to eat,' he said. 'Then we'll go to St Simons and later to Brunswick. All right?'

Paige sat up, ran her fingers through her hair and laughed out of pure joy. It was a gorgeous day, she felt fine, and Chad was with her. Everything was right with the world.

Or was it? Her joyful mood lasted through breakfast, and she hummed as she busied herself with tidying the Sea House while Chad showered and dressed. But when they left the cottage in the Mule, heading towards the Manse, she suddenly felt as though she were leaving her happiness behind. The Sea House had become a symbol of something to her, and while they had stayed there they had been able to shut the rest of the world with its realities out of their lives. Now they were about to take up where they left off.

Sitting next to him in the Mule she was all too aware of his compelling physical presence; she couldn't, however, forget the beauty of their lovemaking last night. Even though they had stopped short of true physical fulfilment, the emotional high had been something special for both of them. But she felt as though a cold hand was clutching her heart when she realised that perhaps she had been living in a dream world where nothing was real, nothing was subjected to the tests and rules that governed their everyday lives. They could no longer be a world unto themselves.

She still had to talk to the aunts about Chad's role in their financial management, and she cautioned herself that she might not like what she found out about him. The mystery about Chad Smith had never been cleared up, and she almost wished she could drop the whole matter and go on living in the dream. Of course, that wasn't possible.

Lost in her thoughts, she scarcely realised that they had pulled up in front of the Manse.

'I'll wait for you on the dock while you get ready,' said Chad. Paige gazed up at him mutely, and reading her as well as he did, he realised that something was wrong. She climbed out of the Mule and ran into the Manse, calling over her shoulder, 'I'll be out soon,' and hurried up to her room. Reality. She already felt as though a chasm had opened between them.

She chose a classic white silk shirt, short-sleeved, with a pintucked border on the sleeves and pocket, and a pair of softly pleated red slacks with a gold mesh belt. She showered quickly, trying not to think about Chad.

She kept her mind on last night, the pure ecstatic enchantment of it. She wondered if Chad were thinking about it, too.

When she had showered and washed her hair and blown it dry, she dressed carefully, and then, favouring her foot only a little, she walked to the dock to meet him. It was a beautiful day without a trace of clouds in the sky; no one would ever guess that St Albans had been buffeted by such terrible weather. Here and there along the path were tree branches that had blown down during the worst of it. Paige wondered how the other sea islands had fared in comparison.

Chad greeted her cheerfully when she approached the boat. It was as though he had made up his mind to act as though he didn't know that she was torn with doubts. He had already removed the tarpaulin from *Paige One*, and she could hear the engine idling.

'You've probably guessed by now why I named the new boat as I did,' he said as he helped her into the ChrisCraft.

'It's a play of words on your actual profession—a clue, if I'd only been clever enough to figure it out.'

'It's also a tribute to you. Do you know how pretty you look this morning? I like that outfit.'

'Thank you,' she replied. 'You're just used to seeing me slopping around the Sea House in your old clothes; anything would be an improvement.'

'You look wonderful all the time,' he told her, and he leaned over and kissed her on the cheek. She smiled up at him; it was almost as it had been for the last few days. Maybe there was hope. Maybe it would last.

The trip to St Simons didn't take long, and when they had docked at the public docks, Chad located a taxi to take them to the doctor's office. Paige had anticipated a problem in seeing the doctor because they had no appointment, but when the receptionist heard Chad's story of the snakebite and their isolation and inability to get to either doctor or hospital, she wedged them into her tight schedule.

The doctor turned out to be a middle-aged man with a sprinkling of grey in his hair, and, while Chad excused himself to use the telephone, he inspected Paige's snakebite. He pushed his glasses back on his nose and said, 'I don't mind telling you that I couldn't have done better myself. Believe me, if a snake ever bites me, I'd want Chad Smith around to take care of it!'

Chad and Paige came out of the doctor's office to find a long black limousine parked at the kerb. Paige was looking down the street, wondering if the taxi had waited, when Chad reached down and opened the limousine's door.

She stared at him, and her mouth dropped open. 'What——!' was all she could manage to say.

'This is why I had to make the phone call. Go ahead, get in,' he ordered with a grin. Somehow Paige sensed that he meant it.

When she hesitated, he grasped her firmly by the arm and bundled her into the car. In the front seat a liveried chauffeur sat staring straight ahead, the personification of dignity.

'Chad, if this is your idea of a joke, please stop.' She shot him a wild-eyed look, stared at the chauffeur, looked back at Chad. Chad sat back in the plush seat, grinning at her. He seemed to be enjoying this.

'If you don't tell me whose car this is, Chad Smith, I'm getting out at the next stop sign. I *mean* it!'

'Actually, the car belongs to W. Chadbourne Smith III. In other words, me.' He resumed the grin, watching her in amusement.

'Be serious, Chad. I don't want jokes.' Her heart was beating faster, and she couldn't understand the smug look on Chad's face.

'I'm more serious than I've ever been,' he assured her, and suddenly she believed that he meant it. But—but this was impossible! She had had him pegged for a boat bum—how could he own a car like this? Something like panic rose in her throat. She felt as though the world were crumbling around her.

'W. Chadbourne Smith III,' she murmured to herself, leaning back in the seat beside him and wrinkling her forehead. She had heard that name before. If only she could think of where! Right now her mind was reeling and she couldn't think of anything at all.

'Does the name ring a bell?'

'Sort of.' She massaged her temples; she hoped she wasn't getting a headache.

'I'll let you think about it a while longer,' said Chad. And then to the chauffeur, 'Take us home, please, Richards.'

Paige stared out at the oak-lined streets. Clean-up crews were busy hauling away dead limbs and clumps of Spanish moss that had blown down in the heavy winds. Here in this limousine with its whisper-soft air conditioning, she felt removed from everything outside. Even the motor made no sound. Chad didn't either.

He was watching her, still grinning like the Cheshire Cat in *Alice in Wonderland*. She wished he'd stop it, wished he'd explain more, but he didn't seem inclined to explain anything.

She looked out her window again. Richards had turned the car on to the causeway leading to exclusive Sea Island. Paige wondered if she were going mad. Chad had told the chauffeur to take him home, and she thought it was impossible that he could live on Sea Island. The houses there were grand, expensive. But then, she reflected, if Chad really owned a chauffeured limousine, anything was possible.

Neither of them spoke until the chauffeur turned the limousine into a concrete driveway spanned by a wrought-iron arch. A gate was set in the arch; Richards opened the limousine's electric window with the touch of a button and reached out and punched a code into a box set in a post, releasing the gate mechanism so that the gate swung slowly open by itself.

'Security system,' Chad explained unnecessarily. The limousine rolled past a high hedge, a goldfish pond, a grape arbour. It pulled up in front of a huge and magnificent house, a stylised chateau much like those Paige had admired on trips through the French countryside.

'Here we are,' said Chad cheerfully. 'Be it ever so humble, there's no place like home.'

Paige was speechless as Richards opened the door for her. Chad opened his own door and hurried around to take her by the elbow. He called over his shoulder, 'Leave the car out, Richards. I'll want it again.' He steered Paige up the steps to the impressive front entrance. An elderly uniformed housekeeper was waiting at the door; she opened it at their approach. She greeted Chad with a wide smile and a charming French accent. 'Welcome home, Mr Smith,' she said, all but curtseying. Paige could feel her mouth dropping open again; she clamped it shut abruptly.

'Ah, Simone,' said Chad. 'This is Miss Brownell. You'll be seeing a lot of her around here.' And to Paige, 'Simone is the one who runs things in this house. Including me.' He put a proprietorial arm around Paige's shoulders and led her through the marble-floored foyer with its Waterford crystal chandelier and great swooping circular staircase, past the dining room, decorated in a delicate shade of rose-petal pink, through the living room with its pearl-grey carpet and off-white upholstery.

When Paige found her voice, she managed to say, 'You don't mean to tell me that this is where you live.'

'Oh, yes I do. Didn't I tell you yesterday that today you would be astonished and amazed? Didn't you believe me?'

'I wasn't prepared for anything like this. I didn't know there were people who still lived this lavishly.' She gazed around her in rapt fascination.

'Take a French heiress—my mother—and marry her

to the grandson of the founder of one of this country's largest steel companies—my father—and you have the ingredients for a life of luxury.'

'Your parents live here?'

'My father died many years ago, and my mother lives in Switzerland with her second husband, an Austrian with a title that I can never remember. So I have this place—and our homes in Vail, Colorado, and Pennsylvania—to myself.'

Paige turned to face him, still finding it hard to believe. 'So why do you live on St Albans? Why don't you live here?'

Chad shook his head. 'When you figure out who W. Chadbourne Smith III really is, you'll understand.'

He was infuriating! she thought in dismay. If only she could recall where she'd heard his name. It seemed to her that he was someone famous, but she couldn't for the life of her think of why.

No time to ponder it now; he had taken her hand and led her to the curtains that were drawn across the window. He pulled them aside to reveal the Atlantic Ocean bordered by a white strip of beach. It was almost as lovely as the beach on St Albans.

'I own it all,' he said, taking in her stupefied look with another grin. 'Except the Atlantic Ocean, of course.'

'Chad, I don't know what to say,' she said lamely. And she didn't. Of course, the revelation that Chad Smith was wealthy shot to ribbons her theory that he was trying to get his hands on her aunts' money. It left her wondering more than ever why her aunts had given him control of their fortune.

'Do my aunts know who you are?' she demanded suddenly, narrowing her eyes at him.

'Of course. When I first met Aunt Biz at the Brunswick dock, I offered to work on St Albans as a handyman just so she'd invite me to live on the island. I'd never as much as hammered a nail before I arrived there. But then when I saw how decrepit it all looked, I tried to help them out as much as I could, even though I felt like I was all thumbs. I let them think that I enjoyed doing odd jobs. At first I didn't mean to tell them who I was, but I found that I couldn't deceive them. I told both Aunt Biz and Aunt Sophie about my millions a week or so after I moved in. I said that I was tired of being W. Chadbourne Smith III, and that I just wanted to be plain ordinary Chad Smith for a while. They accepted it, and me.'

His openness made it unlikely that he was lying. 'If you told them, why didn't you ever tell me?' Paige's mind was galloping, trying to keep up, but she felt as though she were falling hopelessly behind. Things were moving much too rapidly.

Chad put his hands on her shoulders and turned her to face him. He looked deep into her eyes. 'I couldn't tell you, Paige. I didn't want my money to become an issue until I knew how you felt about me. When women find out that I'm wealthy, all sorts of things start to happen. They see my money, not me. I didn't want that to happen with us.'

She shook her head slowly to clear it. 'Wouldn't that have been better than letting me go on thinking what I was thinking? That you were an unmotivated, unemployed vagrant intent on stealing from my aunts?'

Chad threw his head back and laughed. 'No, actually I rather enjoyed the role. Except for the part about stealing from your aunts. I didn't want you to think I was deficient in character, after all. You'd never marry anyone who was an out-and-out blackguard.'

'Marry?' she whispered, not sure she had heard him correctly.

'Yes, my love, marry. As in I'm madly in love with you. But more about that later. You can think it over until then.' He was looking down at her with a twinkle in his eyes, then he was pulling her along behind him as he strode up the circular staircase to the second floor.

I think, Paige thought to herself wildly, I've just received a proposal of marriage. If she'd heard him correctly, he'd said he loved her. And then she felt an almost wild impulse to laugh. This was preposterous, all of it. Like a huge joke. And yet, most preposterous of all, it wasn't a joke.

They reached the upstairs landing and Chad began flinging doors open, tugging her along in his wake.

'Here's the blue bedroom,' he said, showing her a huge bedchamber decorated in pale blue brocade with jonquil yellow accents, then he took her across the hall and showed her the pink bedroom, done entirely in pink moiré with a dove-grey carpet. 'And here's the master bedroom,' he said, throwing the door open upon a gigantic bedroom tastefully decorated in pale green silk with touches of peach. The furniture was French provincial, clearly authentic, and the windows framed a magnificent view of the ocean.

'Actually, the minute I saw your sea-green eyes, I knew you were the wife I wanted,' Chad told her. 'I'd never found anyone who would fit in with the décor of this room as well as you do. You *do* like it, don't you?' he queried, turning to her anxiously.

'Yes, but——' she began faintly. He seemed to take it for granted that she would marry him! She tried to wrap her mind around the idea and failed. It was hard to imagine herself mistress of this house, not to mention his other homes in Pennsylvania and Vail.

'Of course,' Chad was saying as he led her through bathrooms and a sewing room and a room that he said could some day be furnished as a nursery, 'of course, I'll give you carte blanche with the house. You can redecorate it any way you choose.' It was mind-boggling, thought Paige frantically. She couldn't imagine herself living in a place like this, couldn't believe he wanted to marry her, couldn't fully comprehend all the things he was telling her.

They bade a hurried farewell to Simone, Paige feeling tongue-tied, and climbed back into the limousine.

'The dock, Richards,' ordered Chad, and soon they had left the mansion behind.

Chad still held her hand, refusing to let it go. 'So what did you think of the house?' he asked.

'It's beautiful,' she said. 'I just can't make the connection between you and that way of life.' She looked at him helplessly. 'I just can't,' she repeated.

He patted her hand. 'I know, I know, it must be a shock. But brace yourself, because there's more.'

They drew up in front of a dock at a yacht club that looked highly exclusive.

'Now what?' Paige asked apprehensively.

'Now I show you what my life has been about for several years.' They got out of the car and he led her down the length of the dock. At the end of it rose the masts of a sleek racing yacht.

They stopped at the end of the dock and Chad pointed to the name lettered across the narrow stern. '*Dreadnaught*,' read Paige. It was a name that seemed somehow familiar, and then, in a flash, it came to her. '*Dreadnaught*,' she said again, with mounting recognition. She wheeled and stared at Chad. 'Not the *Dreadnought* that won the America's Cup! Surely not!' Her voice had risen in amazement.

Chad nodded proudly. 'That's the one,' he said. 'Isn't she beautiful?'

'But then you're—you're——' she couldn't go on.

'W. Chadbourne Smith III,' he said patiently. 'I told you. You can't imagine how crushed I was that you didn't recognise the name right off. I've grown used to being famous, you know.' There was a little wooden bench near by; Chad led her to it, and they sat down. There was no sound but the water slapping against the dock pilings and against the hull of the yacht *Dreadnaught*.

Paige stared at the face she had come to love so well, the high cheekbones, the amber-flecked eyes, the determined chin with its almost imperceptible cleft. Add a beard and a moustache and he would look exactly like—would *be*—the flamboyant skipper of the racing yacht that had come from behind for a mere ten-second victory over the crack challenging Norwegian yacht, *Trondheim*. Oddsmakers had given the *Dreadnaught* almost no chance to win the ocean race off Newport, Rhode Island.

W. Chadbourne Smith III, the brilliant captain of the *Dreadnaught*, had dominated the news in those days, especially after the world found out that he was a wealthy, eligible bachelor. He had been interviewed on countless television talk shows, been the subject of a segment on TV's *60 Minutes*, appeared on the cover of *Time* magazine. *People* magazine had printed pictures of him with various Hollywood starlets, and for a while he had been the darling of the gossip columnists. Then, suddenly and inexplicably, W. Chadbourne Smith III had disappeared from view. No one knew where he had gone, and before long, no one cared.

'I shaved off the beard and moustache,' Chad explained. 'I got tired of the fast-paced life I was leading after *Dreadnaught* won the America's Cup. Oh, I tried holing up in my condominium in Vail and later in my house in Pennsylvania to write my book, but people got wind of who I was and they wouldn't leave me alone. I came to my house here, thinking that no one would find me, but the phone rang and rang. I got an unlisted number, and reporters still bugged me. So when by chance I met your Aunt Biz and learned that she lived on a secluded island off the coast, unconnected by telephone to the mainland or anywhere else, I knew it was just what I needed. By that time my ambition to write *the* definitive book on yacht racing had become an obsession, and I knew total seclusion was the only way I'd ever be able to finish it.'

'You didn't tell anyone about the book, though. Why?'

'I knew that as soon as the word got out that I was

writing a book, I'd be besieged by media people who were looking for some fresh copy about me. I couldn't take that chance. So, not knowing whether Aunt Sophie and Aunt Biz might drop a hint here and there if they knew about the book, I simply chose not to tell them about it.'

'Or me.'

'Or you. I didn't see how I could tell you about the book without your eventually figuring out that I was the W. Chadbourne Smith III whose name had become synonymous with yacht racing all over the world. And then you'd know how rich I was and everything would change between us.' He smiled at her, slid an arm around her shoulders. The wind fluttered his hair across his forehead in that endearing way. Paige felt herself smiling back.

'And the *Dreadnaught*? Is she always berthed here? I should think she would be a dead giveaway.'

'She's been in dry dock, having some work done. I've had her delivered here because my crew will arrive in a week or so and we're going to take her out and try her. You're right, she's a giveaway, but now it doesn't matter any more. I've finished the book, you see.'

He drew her close to him and kissed her once on the lips. 'Bear with me a little longer,' he said, his lips close to her ear. 'We have one more stop to make, and then we're going back to St Albans.' He stood up and walked her to the limousine, his arm around her shoulders.

Paige was beginning to digest it all, and things were falling into place, she thought as Richards drove them across the causeway and over the marshes to Brunswick. Chad directed the chauffeur to the bank, and when they went inside Paige noticed how the bank employees snapped to attention when Chad walked by. Especially Glynis, who looked glad to see him, until she realised that Chad was with Paige.

'Chad, I have those papers ready,' Glynis began, but Chad cut her off briskly.

'Fine, Glynis, I'll get them later. Right now I want to see Jacob Hightower,' and he strode around Glynis's desk and ushered Paige directly into his office.

Jacob Hightower was talking on the telephone, but when he saw Chad he hung up immediately. He stood up, and unlike the day when Paige had visited him alone, this time his manner was plainly obsequious. 'Why, Mr Smith,' he said with a deferential smile, 'what can we do for you today?'

'Please tell Miss Brownell everything about my financial association with her aunts. Everything,' and Chad pinned him with a meaningful gaze.

Jacob Hightower looked flustered. 'Everything?' he hedged. 'I'm not sure that would be wise.'

'Everything,' insisted Chad in his most commanding tone.

'Miss Brownell, Mr Smith, please sit down,' and Jacob Hightower indicated two chairs. He studied Paige for a moment, and again Paige noted the unfavourable contrast between him and his predecessor, kind Mr Lingfelt.

'I suppose,' he began, 'that it all began several years ago when I became president of the bank. Mr Lingfelt, who had handled your aunts' money for years, retired. Biz and Sophie took his retirement rather hard, I'm afraid. After all, they were used to his way of handling things and they had established a certain rapport that I found hard to follow. In other words, they didn't like dealing with me as much as they did with him.' Jacob Hightower paused and cleared his throat.

Paige didn't doubt that the aunts had found this man difficult to deal with. His very manner was intimidating.

'Little by little, they began to ignore my advice. Biz would pull out large amounts of money and invest it, and to make a long story short, her judgment was poor.

She lost huge amounts of cash, was forced to live off the principal.'

'But surely you tried to stop her when she began to lose money?' Paige found it hard to believe that what she had thought was a huge family fortune had been so depleted.

'Of course, but they are grown women. They wouldn't listen to me. By and by, with inflation and the cost of living, it was almost all gone. There was barely anything left. Your Aunt Biz blamed me, said she couldn't work with me. I felt terrible about it, but what could I do?' Jacob Hightower regarded her gloomily. 'Then Chad Smith came along. I don't mind telling you that he's the best thing that could have happened to your aunts.'

Paige looked from Chad to Jacob Hightower. 'But why?'

'Chad is an astute businessman, Miss Brownell. He manages his own money, knows when to take risks and when *not* to take risks. He and your aunts began discussing finances, and they recognised his expertise. They began following his advice. Before long, they wanted him to manage everything. They're not as young as they used to be; they wanted to be free of the responsibility. They told me that they trust him completely.'

Chad turned to Paige. 'I didn't want to do it, Paige. But when I realised how much financial difficulty they were in, I had to. I couldn't let them go on as they were. They had almost hit rock bottom. So I agreed to manage their money for them.'

'It's a good thing he did, too,' said Jacob Hightower. 'In fact, Chad might not want me to tell you this part of it, but he's been depositing money in their account, and they know nothing of it. If it weren't for him, they might have lost everything—St Albans, the Manse, all of it.'

Paige felt numb. 'I had no idea things were so bad,' she said slowly.

'Your aunts are proud ladies,' Chad said gently. 'They don't go around complaining. Fortunately, they're doing very well now. And will continue to do well.'

'That's only because of Chad,' said Jacob Hightower. 'Around the bank we have a saying. You remember the story about King Midas—everything he touched turned to gold? Well, we say that Chad Smith has the touch of gold. He has almost a sixth sense about money. Your aunts will never have to worry about money again as long as he's in charge.'

Chad rose from his seat. 'Thank you, Jacob,' he said. And to Paige, who had thought that nothing else could surprise her but who was now sitting in her chair feeling very surprised indeed, he said, 'Paige? Shall we go?'

She didn't speak, just walked with him out of the office, past Glynis, outside to the limousine. Richards headed the car back towards St Simons.

'So you see, my dear, I'm not the bad guy you thought I was,' Chad said lightly.

'I hardly know what to say,' Paige said faintly. 'It's true, all of it, it must be, but it's so hard to understand.' She paused for a moment; they rode in silence while she thought about Chad's subscription to the *Wall Street Journal*, which now made perfectly good sense. Then a thought occurred to her. 'The horses,' she said. 'They're *your* horses, aren't they? You don't exercise them for the stable, do you?'

Chad laughed. 'I wondered when you'd figure that out. They're my horses, all right; they board at the stable.'

'I knew they were too beautiful to be stable hacks. But I thought you'd bought them with money that you'd bled from my aunts. You see, I really had a terrible opinion of you.'

'I know,' said Chad, sounding regretful. 'And I realise that this has been a day of shocks for you,' he added soothingly, putting his arm around her and pulling her close to him on the wide plush seat of the limousine. 'We're going back to St Albans now, and we're going to have a nice quiet evening, just the two of us, alone. After all, Aunt Sophie and Aunt Biz will be back soon.'

'I suppose you don't want me to tell them that you've been giving them money all along,' said Paige.

'I wish you wouldn't,' replied Chad. 'It wouldn't do a bit of good and would only get them upset. Anyway, I didn't do it as much for them as I did for myself. It made me happy to do something nice for them, as kind as they've been to me.'

'Touch of gold,' she murmured, nestling close to him. 'Heart of gold, too.' Chad kissed her gently on the forehead.

Back at St Albans, they worked companionably side by side in the kitchen of the Manse to prepare dinner together; between them, everything was as it was during their idyllic interlude in the Sea House. Later, after they had eaten, they sat in the dim twilight on the veranda outside the study, their chairs drawn close, their hands touching.

'You know,' said Chad, 'for a while I doubted that we'd ever get together. You seemed to dislike me so much right from the first.'

'True,' admitted Paige. 'I was concerned about my aunts. Wouldn't you have been, if you'd been in my place?'

Chad considered this. 'Perhaps. All I know is that I was taken with you from the very beginning, from the moment I saw you standing on the dock at St Simons with the wind whipping your hair about your face.'

'I knew you were attracted to me. But then later you turned so cold, as though you didn't like me any more.'

'It was because I wanted you so desperately, and you put me off with your high-minded talk about "communion of the spirit". I decided I'd ignore you, get you out of my system by singlemindedly concentrating on doing those awful chores on your list. It didn't work, of course. I couldn't avoid you, and your beauty drove me to distraction. By then I knew I was falling in love with you.'

'Falling in love with me? Even then?'

'Even then. And when Lee Tracy took you out, I couldn't bear it. I decided that I wouldn't give you a chance to find whatever it was you were looking for with him. And then after Lee Tracy, Stephen McCall dropped out of the sky, and for an awful time I thought you were going to fly away with him. That's when I began to pursue you in earnest. And then *I* found what you were looking for, too.' He smiled at her contentedly.

When it had grown dark and the blue velvet sky had cupped itself over them, swinging the stars so close that they could have reached up and touched one, Chad said, 'Let's walk down to the dock and watch the moon rising over the marsh.'

Paige agreed, and arm in arm they walked down the oyster-shell path, through the sighing trees, and stood on the dock gazing across the shadowy marsh grass at the golden moon lying low in the sky. Stars were reflected in the water, making it seem as though they stood above a rippling blanket of stars; when Paige looked up at Chad, she saw more stars glowing deep in his golden eyes.

He drew her close until she felt his heart beating close to hers. She wrapped her arms around him, loving him, trusting him, wanting him. She felt almost overcome by the intensity of her feelings. W. Chadbourne Smith III, she thought to herself. A few short days ago, she never would have believed it.

Chad's voice sounded heavy with emotion. 'Don't you think you've had long enough to think it over?' he said.

She pulled slightly apart from him, looked up at him. 'Think what over?'

'Marrying me. I believe I mentioned it earlier today.'

'Let's see, I do think I remember something about it. You sandwiched it in rather neatly between the Atlantic Ocean, which you don't own, and all those bedrooms, which you do.'

'Well, what's the answer? You can't expect me to wait for ever, you know.'

'For ever,' she said dreamily, kissing the little cleft in the middle of his chin. 'That's a long time.'

'A very long time,' he agreed, kissing the tip of her nose.

'But not nearly long enough for us,' she said, nibbling at his earlobe, which she could barely reach.

'Still, it's a start,' he said, pressing his lips against her eyelids, one by one.

'A very good start indeed,' she murmured, and pulled his head down until his lips covered hers. And the stars above and below them wrapped them in their luminous glow, and the whole world seemed bright, bright and golden and full of love.

Coming Next Month in Harlequin Romances!

2665 PETER'S SISTER Jeanne Allan
A battle-scarred Vietnam veteran shows up in Colorado and triggers painful memories in his buddy's sister. He reminds her of the brother she lost and the love she's never forgotten.

2666 ONCE FOR ALL TIME Betty Neels
When tragedy strikes a London nurse, support comes — not from her fiancé — but from her supervising doctor. But she finds little comfort, knowing he's already involved with another woman.

2667 DARKER FIRE Morgan Patterson
Because she so desperately needs the job, a Denver secretary lies about her marital status. But how can she disguise her feelings when her boss asks her to leave her husband and marry him instead?

2668 CHÂTEAU VILLON Emily Spenser
Her wealthy French grandfather tries to make amends for having disinherited her father. Instead, he alienates Camille and the winery's heir when he forces them to marry before love has a chance to take root.

2669 TORMENTED RHAPSODY Nicola West
The idea of returning to the tiny Scottish village of her childhood tantalizes and torments a young Englishwoman. Inevitably, she'll run into the man who once broke her heart with his indifference.

2670 CATCH A FALLING STAR Rena Young
Everyone in the music business calls her the Ice Maiden. But there's one man in Australia capable of melting her reserve — if only to sign her with his nearly bankrupt recording company.